LUCIFER'S WEEKEND

LUCIFER'S WEEKEND

DIGGER #4

WARREN MURPHY

OPEN ROAD
INTEGRATED MEDIA
NEW YORK

ISBN 978-1-4976-4238-6

This edition published in 2014 by Open Road Integrated Media, Inc.
345 Hudson Street
New York, NY 10014
www.openroadmedia.com

For Ed and Christine,
Bob and Anna and Billy
and Karen. Friends.

LUCIFER'S
WEEKEND

LOCAL MAN DIES IN MISHAP

BELTON, PENNSYLVANIA—Vernon Gillette, an electronics and planning specialist with Belton and Sons Industries, was discovered dead yesterday morning in a small hunting cabin in the north hill section on the outskirts of the town of Belton.

Police said that Gillette was apparently electrocuted while working on the cabin's electrical system. He had been at the cabin to hunt deer. In the cabin, which is owned by Belton and Sons for the use of their employees, police said they found an electrical fuse next to Gillette's hand. The man's body was lying on the floor in the bathroom.

Gillette, 41, was a native of California and was educated at U.C.L.A. Considered a specialist in the design and operation of electronic information systems, Gillette had several college degrees, including those in electrical engineering and computer systems science. He worked in New York until two years ago, when he moved to Belton to join Belton and Sons.

Gillette is survived by his wife, the former Louise Randisi, and their 8-year-old daughter, Ardath.

Chapter One

"Digger, you have done some disgusting things to me in your life, but this is low, even for you." Walter Brackler looked nervously over his shoulder toward the crowded dance floor.

"What's the matter with dancing?" Digger asked. "I love to see people dancing. I think they're kind of graceful."

"They're men dancing," Brackler said. "With each other." He leaned forward. "It's a fag bar, Digger. A fag bar," he whispered angrily, before sitting up straight and glancing over his shoulder again.

Julian Burroughs shook his head. "No, no," he said. "It's a 'gay' bar, not a fag bar."

"What's the difference?"

"Fourteen leather jackets and twenty pounds of chains," Digger said. "Seventy-eight key rings, ninety-seven switchblade knives and fourteen thousand arrests for loitering."

"I should have known," Brackler said glumly. "When I got here, I looked at the outside of this place and I said to myself, Julian Burroughs is getting mellower. Usually, I have to meet you in these terrible grungy places, but this place looked clean. I thought, maybe Digger will not be on the snot today. Maybe we will transact our business like real human beings and I will leave this place not hating him. Not a chance. You are a despicable human being."

"If you play your cards right, I can fix you up," Digger said. He drained his glass of vodka and waved toward the waiter for another round.

"None for me," Brackler said. "Who knows what they do with the glasses when the customers aren't looking?"

"Wash them, I suspect," Digger said. "So what's on your mind?"

"And the music is awful, too," Brackler said.

"You're not into Marlene Dietrich impersonations?"

"So loud? Does it have to be so loud?"

"If it weren't loud, you wouldn't be able to hear it over the panting and slurping," Digger said.

"Disgusting. This is absolutely the last time I meet you anyplace except in the offices of Brokers Surety Life Insurance Company. That is my last fucking word on the subject," Brackler said.

"This place has Finlandia vodka," Digger said.

"Who gives a shit?" Brackler said.

"I'm sorry you're so offended," Digger said. "I thought you knew it was a gay bar."

"How would I know that?" Brackler asked.

"By the name. Danny's. Give me a bar named Danny's and two times out of three, it's a gay bar. That's a proven fact. I thought you knew that. I thought everybody knew that."

"I don't have your deep knowledge of the seamy underside of life," Brackler said. He saw the waiter returning, mincing across the floor with a drink tray in his hand, so he turned slightly in his chair, then pressed closer to the wall. The waiter set two drinks on the table and removed the empties. He smiled at Digger, then at Brackler, before turning away.

"He thinks you're the cutest little thing," Digger told Brackler.

"Work, right? Here. Read this." Brackler took a newspaper clipping from his inside jacket pocket and handed it to Digger, who unfolded it and lay it flat in his left palm to read, while raising his glass of vodka to his lips with his right hand.

Digger glanced off to the right and saw their waiter staring at their table. He was struck by how much the waiter reminded him of a younger Walter Brackler. Both were barely five feet tall, small boned and delicate. Except the waiter was friendlier. Everybody was friendlier to Digger than Walter Brackler.

"The clipping, Digger," Brackler said.

Digger's eyes flickered down to the paper for a few seconds, then back up to meet Brackler's.

"All right, so Vernon Gillette died in an electrical accident. I take it he was insured by 'your company," Digger said.

"*Our* company as long as you live off our paychecks," Brackler said. "Yes, that's correct."

"A large policy," Digger said.

"Correct again."

"And you want me to go up there and prove it was suicide so that you don't have to pay, you cheap bastards," Digger said. "Or is it *we* cheap bastards?"

"Wrong," Brackler said. "We want to pay."

Digger clapped both hands to his chest. "I don't know if my heart can stand the strain." He looked up to the ceiling. Small light bulbs embedded in the blue stucco ceiling twinkled, like stars in a nighttime sky. But there were six crescent moons on the ceiling. What kind of sky had six moons? Maybe homosexual heaven would have a moon for everybody.

"Try to bear up while I explain it to you," Brackler said.

"All right, but no more sudden shocks," Digger said.

"Vernon Gillette had a large policy with us. A half a million dollars, paid for by Belton and Sons. Of course, it is double that for an accidental death."

"So you owe Mrs. Gillette a million dollars," Digger said.

"Your mathematics are, as ever, impeccable," Brackler said.

"So pay up," Digger said. He shook his head. "I don't understand you insurance people. Insurance is a gamble. It's like a game and you're the casino. When people live, you win, and when they die, you lose. And you win some and you lose some, but the casino always wins in the long run and you guys always get your tenor twenty-or eighty-percent profit or whatever it is you're gouging out of your victims right now. So why is it that you hate to pay off ever? That you want to win every hand? What's wrong with you people? God, I hate insurance men."

"I love it when you jump to conclusions," Brackler said, "because it shows how narrow-minded and anti-establishment you truly are. The fact, Mr. Julian Burroughs, social critic extraordinary, is that we want to pay. We want to pay Mrs. Gillette one million dollars."

"Damn it, Kwash, that's wonderful," Digger said. "Just for that, I'm going to buy you another drink."

"I told you I won't drink out of their glasses," Brackler said. "I haven't even touched this one."

"I'll buy you your own bottle. You can drink right out of the bottle. There's not much they can do with a bottle. At least a full one," Digger said.

"I'll pass. Let's just conclude our business so I can get out of here," Brackler said.

"All right," Digger said. He cleared his throat, sat up straight in his chair and folded his hands on the table in front of him like an attentive schoolboy. "Tell me how your willingness to pay somebody a million dollars is any business of mine. Tell me how this guy's accident is any business of mine. Tell me what we're doing here."

"We want to pay the million, but the dead guy's wife…"He snatched the clipping off the table and looked at it again. "…This Mrs. Gillette won't let us. She says that it's insulting to her husband's memory to suggest that he was so stupid that he'd electrocute himself changing a fuse or something. She says he was an electrical genius and he couldn't possibly die that way. Her words, not mine."

"A noble woman," Digger said. He raised his glass in a toast. "If you went right now to my ex-wife's house and told her that I died by driving carpet tacks into my own skull with a sledgehammer, she'd believe you. This Mrs. Gillette's quite a lady."

"She's a gone job," said Brackler, "but that's not here or there. She says that her husband must have died of a heart attack. She won't take a penny more than five hundred thousand dollars."

"So pay her the five hundred thou," Digger said. "You and I can split the rest. We'll buy this place—every place named Danny's is for sale—and we'll turn it into a hairdressing salon. You can handle the gay trade, I'll take care of the women. What do you say?"

Brackler expressed his opinion with a silent stare, cold enough to kill death. Digger said, "Okay, we'll cut Frank Stevens in for some. Not that he needs it. I mean, he's the president of BSLI and he can steal all he wants without stealing from what you and I steal, but if you want to cut him in 'cause he's the boss, all right."

"This is serious," Brackler said.

"So pay the lady, Kwash. What do you want from me? Hand her the check myself? There's a guy over there making eyes at you."

Brackler carefully did not turn around to look. "Which one?" he asked.

"The one that looks like a walking tattoo parlor. With the leather dog collar around his neck."

"Oh, my God," Brackler said. "I've got to get out of here."

"Business, first," Digger said. "How quick you people are to forget what's important. What do you want from me?"

"We can't pay her just the five hundred thou when she's due a million. She might turn around later and sue us for our shirts," Brackler said.

"So you want me to go out there, to Belton... where the Jesus is Belton, what state?"

"Pennsylvania."

"So you want me to go to Belton, PA, and convince this dingdong to take an extra half a million dollars."

"Exactly," Brackler said.

Digger drained his glass of vodka. "Not a chance," he said.

"Why not?"

"First of all, where's Belton, PA?"

"It's about fifty miles north of Pittsburgh," Brackler said.

"That's one reason," Digger said. "I'm not flying into Pittsburgh. Not now, not ever. Not even for you."

"Do you mind telling me what you have against Pittsburgh?"

"I don't have anything against Pittsburgh. It's that goddamn airport in Pittsburgh. You know how in airports things are nice and they have pretty little signs and they say rest room this way or rest room that way?"

"I suppose so," Brackler said cautiously.

"Well, in Pittsburgh Airport, they've got these big blue-and-white signs and they say toilet. That's tacky. It's like having some guy scream over the loudspeaker, 'This way to the crapper.'"

"That's ridiculous," Brackler said.

"Tell the people who run Pittsburgh Airport," Digger said, "not me. And another thing. Everybody in Pittsburgh Airport wears a cowboy hat. It looks like the freaking O.K. Corral. I always figure I'm gonna get involved in a goddamn gunfight. What's that old song? 'Red, white and blue.' Red-neck, white socks and Blue Ribbon beer. No thank you, you go to Pittsburgh."

"You can drive," Brackler said. "Skip the airport. The company will rent a car for you."

"You know how long a drive it is?" Digger asked.

"Yes. It's three hundred ninety-seven miles, one way."

"Which means you had somebody else drive out there," Digger said.

"That's right."

"And?" Digger asked.

"This Mrs. Gillette's elevator does not go to the top floor," Brackler said. "Only you can talk to her."

"She's a loony tune and I don't deal with loony tunes," Digger said. "Present company excepted, of course. That's reason two. Although the Pittsburgh Airport ought to be enough by itself for anybody."

"Digger, you work for me," Brackler said.

"Not really, Kwash. I work for Old Benevolent and Saintly. Occasionally. I was hired by Frank Stevens, our noble president. I guess if I work for anybody, it's for him. Scratch me. Send out another one of your army of assistants, with perfect teeth and wonderful table manners. They sell insurance, they ought to be able to sell Mrs. Gillette on taking another half a million dollars. Hell, if you can sell insurance, you can get anybody to do anything."

Brackler smiled slightly, a narrow little smile that barely touched the corners of his lips and left his eyes inviolate. Digger didn't know what obsidian was, but he knew he was looking into obsidian eyes.

"Frank Stevens himself said that this was a job for you," Brackler said smugly. "The president of Old Benevolent and Saintly, as you like to call it."

"Balls," Digger said in disgust. He waved to the waiter for another drink. "Maybe you misunderstood him. What did he say exactly?"

"He said that if anyone could convince that crazy broad to take an extra five hundred thousand dollars, it would be that crazy Irish bastard. That's a direct quotation."

"Maybe he meant somebody else," Digger said. "I'm only half Irish. I'm half Jewish too, you know."

"He meant you. The word 'crazy' left no doubt about it. So I will tell him you're going to get right on it?"

"Come on, Kwash, cut me a break. This isn't the kind of work I do. Give me natural deaths that are really murders. Give me homicidal maniacs. People killing people for insurance money. Not this. I don't do charm all that well."

This time Brackler's smile reached his eyes and beyond that, his hairline. "But Mr. Stevens specified that *you* should go."

"Oh, this gives you great pleasure, doesn't it?" Digger said. "Watching me squirm? Well, I'll squirm. I'll beg and plead. Kwash, don't send me to Belton, PA. No one's ever gone to Belton, PA, and been heard of again. I'm begging you."

"Go," said Brackler.

"You want me to crawl? I'll crawl." Digger stood up from the table. He was six feet three and casually dressed in a sports jacket and slacks. Somehow, they looked rumpled on him. "I'll crawl. I'll get on my knees and beg." He looked around. "Well, if I get on my knees, I may never get out of this place. Imagine I'm begging."

"You're going to Belton to see Mrs. Gillette," Brackler said.

"I'm going to do it, Kwash," said Digger. "But only as a favor to you. You owe me one and I want you to remember it when I come in the middle of the night for your firstborn."

"Do it for whatever reason you want. Just do it," Brackler said. He handed Digger a manila envelope. "Everything is in here. Keep in touch. And will you please sit down? People are staring at you."

Digger looked around slowly at the crowded cocktail lounge. "They're looking at me," he told Brackler, "but only because they figure they can use me to get close to you." He sat down. "Kwash, you'd be a star in this place. Everybody wants what passes for your body."

"I'm getting out of here," Brackler said. "Stay in touch with me."

"I will," Digger said. "I'm going to mail my reports here to Danny's. They'll hold them until you come to pick them up."

"A telephone call will suffice," Brackler said.

"How'd you ever get to be a vice-president anyway?" Digger asked.

"Working hard, staying honest, doing my best, not rocking the boat. You might try those things, Burroughs."

"On the whole, I'd rather be in Belton, PA," Digger said.

He watched Brackler walk quickly toward the front door, a precise little man in a precise little suit with a precise little haircut and a precise little mind.

The waiter returned with Digger's fresh vodka.

"Your friend left?" he said. He sounded sad.

"Yes," Digger said.

"He seemed like a nice man."

"He is," Digger said. "But he's not into the bar scene. I'll tell you, though, he couldn't keep his eyes off you. He was wondering if you and he could...well, you know, maybe meet sometime outside of here."

"Sure, we could," the waiter said.

Digger pulled a business card from his pocket and wrote on the back of it.

"Here," he said. "Here's his name and address. Walt Brackler. Give him a call. He'd really like to hear from you. He'd really like to be open, out in the life like us, but, well, you know, it comes hard for some people."

The waiter pocketed the card and nodded. "I'll be sure to call him," he said. Then he graced Digger with a smile. "But that still leaves tonight," he said. "You know, your friend's small and I like that, but I like big men too. Big, tall, blond men." He reached his hand tentatively toward Digger's hair.

Digger caught the man's hand and winked at him.

"Tell me," Digger said. "You like travel?"

"Oh, yeah."

"Do you like sex?" Digger asked.

"Of course."

Digger squeezed the waiter's hand hard. "Good. Then take a fucking hike," he said.

Chapter Two

As he drove past the highway sign that read Belton Town Limits, Digger smiled. He had been smiling much of the way from New York, because Walter Brackler had been tricked.

Digger wanted to go to Belton. He could never have told Brackler that, because it would have spoiled the purity of the moment. But Digger's girl friend, Koko, was in Pennsylvania visiting relatives, and Digger thought it would be nice to hook up with her for a couple of days someplace other than Las Vegas, where they shared a condominium apartment.

A glance at his speedometer gave Digger another smile. It wasn't 397 miles to Belton. It was only 391. Digger decided he would be sure to report this to Brackler. If one of Brackler's henchmen had driven out here and billed the company for a 397-mile trip, that was six extra miles. On a round trip, twelve. At twenty cents a mile, that would mean he had beaten the company out of two dollars and forty cents. Digger didn't like people cheating on their expenses because it left that much less for him when it was time for him to cheat on his expenses.

He thought about that for a while, then decided it sounded too much like Corporate Man Goes to Fink School. Instead he would tell Brackler that it was 411 miles to Belton, PA, and that Brackler's man had underbilled him for 14 miles, 28 round trip, and Brackler owed him $5.60 and it was no wonder nobody liked him because he was a cheap bastard and why didn't he pay his man the $5.60 he owed him?

The thought of the coming conversation cheered him and he

stayed cheered until he drove into Belton. The town was shaped like a bowl, and in one corner of the bottom of the bowl was the plant of Belton and Sons, belching smoke, air pollution and God knew what else into the air, from which they dropped down on the population. As he drove down the main street, Digger knew who the longtime residents of the town were because they all squinted and coughed a lot.

Route 8 took him through the center of town, then headed up again toward one of the edges of the bowl. A mile past the heart of Belton, he saw a sign that directed him toward Gus's LaGrande Inn. He had chosen the place solely for the beauty of its name, and he expected linoleum floors, a bathroom in the hall and unlimited coffee privileges at a diner two miles down the road.

What he got instead as he turned off Route 8 was an elegant old estate with sweeping lawns and stately baronial buildings of old, faded red brick.

He followed the twisting road upward until it stopped at a circular drive in front of an old mansion.

Digger parked and carried his own bag inside the building. He was in a large central hallway, and no one else was in sight.

He heard a noise down a hallway toward the right, left his bag on the floor under a small table on which rested a vase of real cut flowers and walked down the hallway. He saw a young man with a thin dark moustache standing behind a counter. A telephone was propped between his shoulder and ear. As he talked he riffled through a stack of bills. When Digger drew closer, he saw that there was a round bar, with about a dozen stools, behind the young man. Farther down the hall, Digger heard the faint buzz of conversation and the tinkling of cutlery and glasses.

It was lunchtime at Gus's LaGrande Inn.

The young man with the moustache put down the stack of bills and, still mumbling into the phone, turned to a low, small section of the bar next to him and began concocting a pitcher of whiskey-sour mix.

Digger waited in front of the counter. The man kept talking into the phone. Digger cleared his throat and the man turned toward him.

"Just a minute," he said into the phone. He said to Digger, "Can I help you?"

"I'm checking in."

"It'll be a few minutes," the man said.

"I'll wait at the bar," Digger said.

"That won't do any good," the young man said. "I'm the bartender too."

Digger shook his head. "I don't mind waiting to check into a motel, but I won't be kept waiting at a bar."

"What are you drinking?"

"Finlandia."

"What's that?"

Digger sighed. He should have known better. After all, this was Belton, PA. "Never mind," he said. "Vodka, rocks."

The young man scooped a glass full of ice, turned and slid it down the bar toward one of the seats. He handed Digger a bottle of house-brand vodka.

"Here," he said, "help yourself. We'll square away when I get all this shit taken care of."

"You've got a future in this business," Digger said.

"I hope so. My past is already buried in it," the young man said, and turned back to his telephone conversation, his mixing of drinks for waitresses who appeared with liquor orders for their lunch tables, and his checking the stack of bills.

It didn't take as long as Digger had expected because he had had only three drinks before the young man finally came down the bar toward him. During that period a dozen people had walked down the hall, past the bar and toward the front door. They were sleek and fat, but the women were unjeweled, which might be what differentiated Belton's upper classes from the upper classes of big cities, Digger thought. He also thought fleetingly of his bag in the hall, but decided that it was safe. That was another thing that distinguished places like Belton from the real world. People didn't just steal things because they happened to be there.

"Okay," the young man said. "I'm sorry but you caught me right in the middle of lunch rush."

"I think you ought to send a petition to the owner and get

some help," Digger said. "Bartender, reservations clerk, telephone operator, bookkeeper—that's a couple of hats too many."

"It won't work."

"Why not?" Digger asked.

"I'm the owner. Gus LaGrande," the young man said and extended a cold, bony hand for Digger to shake.

Digger shook it. "Julian Burroughs. I called yesterday for a room."

"Oh, yeah. Right. We've got you all fixed up. You've got the best room in the place."

"Does it have its own air supply?"

"What do you…oh, the smog," Gus LaGrande said.

Digger nodded. "How do you breathe with all this crap in the air? It's like being on the beach and having to pick sand out of your teeth."

Gus had picked up a reservation form from the small counter at the end of the bar and he brought it back with a pen for Digger to fill it out.

"The crap in the air is courtesy of Lucius Belton," said Gus. "Pretty easy choice though."

"What's that?" asked Digger.

"You want to breathe or eat? Nearly everybody in this damn town…hell, three towns around, works for Belton and Sons. There's nobody left to bitch about the smoke in the air. They all work for him. I always wanted to write a letter to Ralph Nader and have him come down here with a lot of long-haired lawyers with sinus conditions, and maybe they'd file a federal suit against Belton."

Digger was filling out the reservation card. Under "company" he wrote "none, yet."

Without looking up, he said, "Doesn't sound like you like Lucius Belton much."

"No, he's all right," Gus said. "But I can say whatever I want. It's a luxury, but I guess I'm the only person in town that he doesn't own or who doesn't owe him money. Screw him. I'm independently impoverished. I don't need him."

"I don't know why you got into the hotel business," Digger said. "You should have gotten the gas mask concession."

"I know, but my father just wasn't smart. He ran a construction company around here and he got into a big housing development as a partner with some guy. Well, the development went bust and my father's business went down the tubes. But as part of his payoff, he wound up with this place. He ran it until he died and then he left it to me. He couldn't run a hotel any better than he ran a construction company."

"Nice place, though," Digger said.

"It's a nut house," Gus said. "I've got nine dining rooms and eight guest rooms. I can sleep sixteen people here and I can feed three hundred sixty. I've got a disco over in one of the other buildings. I own thirty acres. I'd put in a golf course, but who wants to play golf on the side of a hill? Maybe I'll put in a pitch and putt course. I've got everything else here except a way to make a living."

"Jesus Christ, if you keep making me depressed, it'll drive me to drink," Digger said.

Gus looked at the once-full bottle in front of Digger. "More like a walk than a drive," he said. He took Digger's registration card and glanced at it. "What are you doing up here anyway, if you don't mind my asking? Belton doesn't get many people just stopping because they had this sudden urge to breathe smoke."

"An insurance problem," Digger said vaguely. "I've got to see a Mrs. Gillette."

Gus said, "Gillette? Gillette? Sorry, I don't know any Gillettes."

"No problem," Digger said. "It's all technical insurance bullshit anyway. How long's your bar open at night?"

"You'd never know it by looking at it now but we do a pretty good bar business at night. I'm open till two o'clock. What was that stuff you asked for before?"

"Finlandia. It's vodka."

"Never heard of it," Gus said. He looked at the registration card again. "Ahhh, you're only staying one day. If you were going to be here awhile, I'd order you some."

"Try anyway," Digger suggested. "You never know, I might be back."

Digger had another drink, then took his room key from Gus and carried his own bag up the curving central staircase to the second floor. When he pushed open the door, he whistled involuntarily. The room was bigger than the main floor of many houses. It held two fireplaces, two full-sized beds, a sofa, an unstocked bar, a round wooden dining table with four chairs, a crystal chandelier and three dressers. The bathroom alone was bigger than most normal motel rooms.

From the living room, he looked through floor-to-ceiling windows out from the hill on which Gus's stood, over a rolling gentle valley that would have been bucolically beautiful if it weren't for the dirty gray mist that filled up the bottom of the bowl.

Lucius Belton, whoever he was, deserved shooting. Or hanging, Digger decided.

But up above the smoke line, Belton was beautiful, and, as Digger looked around, he could see homes clustered all around the upper sides of the valley.

It was just early afternoon, and Digger decided that he would shower first, call Koko, then go see Mrs. Gillette and maybe, before nightfall, he would be out of Belton, PA, on his way to see Koko.

Still damp after his shower, Digger lay on the bed and called the home of Koko's family in Emporium, Pennsylvania.

The telephone was answered in the middle of the first ring. Digger recognized the accented voice of Koko's mother.

"Hello, Mrs. Fanucci, this is Digger."

"Ah, Digger. So?"

As he usually did when he heard her limping English, Digger smiled. The name Mrs. Fanucci conjured up an image of some leviathan of a starch factory, wearing a red-and-green flowered apron, whipping up three million pounds of pasta in a basement kitchen. But this Mrs. Fanucci, Koko's mother, was a trim and tiny Japanese woman who got her American citizenship and her name when she married an American sailor after World War II.

"Is Tamiko there?" Digger asked.

"Yes," the woman said. That was all, nothing more. Digger felt that she would let him hang on forever, because she was too polite to hang up.

After a few seconds, Digger said, "Can I talk to her?"

"No."

"Why not?"

"She's doing the bathroom in the toilet."

"Can I hold on?"

"Can you hold on to what?"

"To the telephone," Digger said.

"Tamiko puts the phone up her shoulder. She makes cookies, the phone up her shoulder. She not hold on. You have to hold on?"

"No," Digger said.

"So do I," Mrs. Fanucci said. "I learn put phone up my shoulder. You want see?"

"Yes, honorable mother," Digger said.

He heard a rustling sound and then a clatter as the telephone hit the floor.

A moment later, Mrs. Fanucci said, "I not do it so good like Tamiko still. I am glad you not see me drop it on floor. I so embarrassed, I kill myself. Here is Tamiko. She is all done in toilet because I hear it flash. Here, Tamiko. Here is Digger. We're having nice talk about the toilet."

"Hello, Digger," said a happy, lilting woman's voice. "Mamma-san been spilling my toilet secrets?"

"Everything but number one or number two," Digger said.

"Number three," Koko said. "A shampoo."

"Why don't you send that woman to Berlitz?" Digger asked.

"Digger, she already knows how to threaten suicide in a language and a half. I couldn't take well-written suicide notes in English. Besides, if she spoke any better, she'd take a run at you herself. It's only the language barrier that's keeping the two of you apart."

"I'm signing up for Japanese lessons in the morning," Digger said. "I always liked her better than you anyway."

"Mutt. Anyway, how's Las Vegas? You miss me yet?"

"It's only been ten days, nine hours and sixteen minutes. Why should I miss you? Besides, I'm not in Las Vegas. That's today's surprise."

"Where are you?"

"I'm in Belton, PA."

"What are you doing there?"

"I've got to see some woman on insurance business, then I thought I might get to see you."

"When?" she asked.

"I don't know. Tonight? Maybe tomorrow?"

"Oh, Digger, not tomorrow," she said.

"Why not?"

"My sister's going into the hospital tomorrow. She might need an operation."

"Again? That girl is always almost, maybe, needing an operation. She's got more goddamn plumbing problems than the public works department in Venice."

"I'm sure she doesn't like it any better than you do," Koko said.

"I think she gets off on sympathy," Digger said. "Anyway I could come and maybe help. Hold everybody's hand. Make small talk and jokes. Keep your mother's spirits up."

"Not tomorrow, Digger. Let's talk tomorrow and see."

"You sure you just don't have a heavy date tomorrow? A school reunion or something and you're embarrassed to have your friends see me?"

"You know better than that. What kind of town is Belton?"

"I've been in a thousand towns like this one," Digger said, suddenly depressed and feeling sorry for himself. "It's always drunk out."

"Don't be maudlin," she said. "You're not unloved. Where are you staying?"

"That's why I thought you might even want to come and visit me. I'm at this beautiful estate. Rolling hills. Horseback riding stables. Swimming pools. A golf course. Everything including smog. Two fireplaces in the bedroom."

"Horses?"

"Absolutely," Digger said. "I saw a dozen lalapaloo-zas in the yard."

"That's appaloosas, idiot," she said. "I love horseback riding."

"If you come and visit me, I'll pay for your first hour. You pay for your second hour yourself," he said.

"After I straighten this out with my sister," Koko said. "What's the name of the place you're at?"

"Gus's LaGrande Inn."

"What?"

"Gus's LaGrande Inn."

"Hey, Dig, I've been there."

"I thought you were never in Belton, PA," he said.

"I didn't know it was in Belton," Koko said. "I went there after my high school senior prom. We were starting away on a class weekend trip."

"Trust you to find a motel," Digger said.

"I really don't need this bullshit," Koko said.

"I'm sorry. Tell me about your prom and Gus's LaGrande Inn."

"My date and I went there after our prom party. It's the first time I ever gave it up. I was almost eighteen."

"Don't tell me about it," Digger said.

"I won't. What room are you staying in?"

"Two-oh-seven. Upstairs."

"Big chandelier in the middle of the room?" she asked.

"Yes, if you want to call it big," Digger said glumly. Big? It was the biggest chandelier he'd ever seen outside of Lincoln Center for the Performing Arts and nine Puerto Rican hotels.

"Look carefully," Koko said. "Is there a red crystal droplet in part of the chandelier near the door? It's red, like one of the other pendants broke and all they had to replace it with was a red one."

Digger glanced up. "Yeah," he said.

"Dig, that's the room. That's where I first got laid."

"I hope the room's as lucky for me," Digger said.

"You poor miserable benighted soul," Koko said. "You're jealous."

"I'm not jealous."

"Of course you are. But how can you be jealous of Hugo Stockelbrinner? He had acne and buck teeth."

"And you," Digger said.

"An act of mercy," Koko said.

"An act of lechery," Digger said. "You people are disgusting."

"Call me tomorrow, Digger," she said. "I'll tell you all about it."

"I'm sure you will," Digger groused, as Koko hung up.

Digger decided to forgo his afternoon visit to Louise Gillette and he decided to forgo dinner too. Instead he dressed and went to the bar.

There was still nobody else at the bar except Gus LaGrande, bartender, waiter, room clerk, bellhop, accountant and owner.

His face brightened when he saw Digger, and he reached under the bar and held up a bottle of Finlandia vodka.

"Look what I got. I was talking to a friend of mine and I

mentioned it and he had some so he sent over a bottle. Hey, you don't look happy."

"I'm only moderately happy."

"Why?"

"One bottle won't be enough. I'm drinking for two."

One bottle wasn't enough. When he closed the bar at 2:15 A.M., having drunk in solitary splendor all night, the bottle of Finlandia was empty and so was much of another bottle of cheap bar vodka.

He finished out the evening by raising his voice in song:

"So make it one for Hugo Stockelbrinner, the acned, beaver-toothed prick...

"And one more for the road."

Digger hung the Do Not Disturb sign on the door to keep the maid at bay, and so he slept until 11:00 A.M. When he woke up and glanced at his watch, he was pleased with himself. Usually, he slept fitfully, grabbing sleep in three-and four-hour snatches. An eight-hour unbroken sleep was an event in his life.

He felt still better after a shower. His head was clear. He had no hangover, although that didn't mean anything since he never had a hangover. He had decided early hi life that this was a mixed blessing. On the one hand, it meant he didn't have to pay a next-day price for his excessive drinking. On the other hand, it had just made it that much easier for him to become an alcoholic.

Digger had thought once of how to head off the next generation of alcoholics. It would be simple. Congress should pass a law requiring a small amount of Antabuse to be mixed with every bottle of liquor sold. Antabuse was the anti-alcohol drug used in clinics; after taking it, people got violently ill if they drank alcohol.

A little Antabuse might head off a whole generation of lushes, Digger thought. He confided this in a letter to his congressman, who wrote back, thanking him for this thoughtful suggestion, promising to look into it and commending Digger for his interest in the governmental process, because without such active citizen participation no government could succeed and the spark of freedom would die in the world.

In other words, the congressman hadn't read Digger's letter.

Digger wasn't discouraged. His was an idea ahead of its time. Its day would come.

His good mood lasted until he started to get dressed and he realized he would not be able to postpone it any longer. He would have to go to see Louise Gillette today. From the bottom of his big suitcase he took out a small pocket-sized tape recorder and attached it to his bare right side with two strips of surgical tape from a roll he kept in his shaving bag. He might as well record the ravings of this woman who was going to turn down a half million of Old Benevolent and Saintly's money. After dressing, he put on a bright red-and-black regimental striped tie and fastened to it a gold tie clip, designed like a frog with an open mouth. It was a singularly ugly tie clip, but it was unique, for a wire ran around from the back of it, under Digger's shirt and connecting into his tape recorder. The open mouth of the frog was covered with a thin mesh, under which was a tiny but high-powered omnidirectional microphone. Digger had had the gadget made when he had gone on his first case for Brokers Surety Life Insurance Company. He traveled nowhere without his tape recorder. One never knew when one might need it; he always seemed to.

Dressed, he looked out his window. The residual haze still hung over the downtown section of Belton at the bottom of the bowl, but at this elevation the air was clean and fresh. He opened his window and breathed deeply and coughed. He smoked four packs of cigarettes a day; now he should start worrying about air pollution? He cheerfully accused himself of being a hypocrite, cheerfully agreed that the accusation was right on the mark and went downstairs.

Gus was mixing drinks behind the bar, but he took a moment out when Digger fished Vernon Gillette's insurance application from his inside jacket pocket and asked him how to find the house.

"North Church Street," Gus said. "That's across the bowl. You can either drive down into the town and then up the other side or you can drive around the edge of the bowl."

"Which way's quicker?" Digger asked.

"Down into town. The main drag is Church Street. You just follow it through town and then up the other side. When you get

above the smoke, start looking for numbers. This number should
be pretty high up."

"Thanks. I'll see you later," Digger said.

"You staying another night?"

"I don't know. Yeah," Digger said. "Keep me booked up. I hate
to have to hurry things."

Driving through the town, Digger figured out how Belton
worked. At the bottom of the bowl were the stores, movie houses,
offices and the homes of the proletariat, hidden under the
continuous haze generated by the Belton and Sons industrial works
at one end of the bowl. As you spiraled upward out of the bowl and
away from the smog, you got to the better residential districts, and
the nearer you got to the top of the bowl, the more expensive the
homes became.

The Gillette family lived about three quarters of the way up the
bowl in a house that was about two windows and two hundred feet
of elevation short of being a mansion.

Digger parked on Church Street in front of the big yellow
stucco structure, hoping he could wrap everything up neatly, then
call Koko and let her apologize for his bad temper, and then spend
some time with her, without invoking the memory of Humphrey
Stickel-maker, or whatever his name was.

When he got out of the car, he looked down the road he had just
driven along. The smog made the center of town almost invisible
and Digger began to wonder if Louise Gillette wasn't turning
down a half million dollars, not because of her husband's memory
but just because living in Belton, PA, had driven her crazy.

Lucius Belton might own the town and almost everyone in it,
but if this had been a Caribbean island, right now there would be
rebels massing in the hills to overthrow him. Digger had an idea
for a movie. *The Revenge of the Smog People*. Film it in Belton. Pay
off all the townspeople with bottles of air flown in from the outside.

Digger rapped once, hard, on the big heavy oak door with the
brass knocker, which sounded like Big Ben, and after a moment the
door slid open easily and quietly. A small girl stood in the doorway.
She was blond and her eyes were a brilliant green. Her long hair
was done up in two braids that hung down over her shoulders. Her
T-shirt read "Save the Whales" and her jeans had raised piping

around the pockets and down the outside seams. She was barefoot and held one hand behind her back.

"Hello," she said.

"Hi," Digger said. "Is the lady of the house in?"

"Oh, dear. You're not selling anything, are you?"

"No. Why?" Digger asked.

"Because my mother is busy. Only certain things are important enough to interrupt her for. Salesmen aren't one of them. I'm empowered to deal with salesmen."

Digger remembered from the newspaper obituary on Gillette that Ardath Gillette was eight years old. Did eight-year-olds talk like this nowadays? Maybe this wasn't Ardath, but a midget maid?

"Are you Ardath Gillette?" Digger asked.

"Yes. Who are you?"

"My name is Julian Burroughs."

"That's very interesting," the girl said.

"Why?"

"Because Julian is probably a Catholic name. But Burroughs is usually Anglo-Saxon and not Catholic. What are you? So you have two names that suggest two different things? What are you?"

"I'll give you a clue. I'm half Jewish."

"Oh, my, you are a very complicated man." Digger noticed that she still had her right hand on the doorknob and her left hand behind her back.

"Actually, I'm very simple," Digger said. "To know me is to see right through me. The incredible transparent man, that's me. What kind of a name is Ardath?"

"That's interesting too. When my parents gave me that name, they thought it was Welsh because they once had a Welsh friend named Ardath. But I looked it up and my name is from the Hebrew. It means flowering fields. Isn't that interesting?"

"Inordinately," Digger said.

"We're both very complex individuals," Ardath said.

"Too bad," Digger said. "I like simple women."

"I don't believe that for a moment. Your eyes laugh, and men whose eyes laugh like life to be complicated. My father had eyes that laugh."

"Ardath," said Digger, "I think I'm falling in love with you. We'd better get on with our business before I stick you in my pocket and run off with you."

The girl seemed, for a moment, to consider Digger's offer.

"It would never work," she said solemnly.

"The age difference?" Digger said.

"I don't really think age matters much," she said. "No. You have the look of a possessive man and I don't think I could let you stand in the way of my career."

"What career is that?" Digger asked.

"How would I know? I'm only eight. You just said, get on with our business. What is 'our business'?"

"I'm with the Brokers Surety Life Insurance Company," Digger said.

"Oh. The insurance company. She won't take it, you know."

"Take what?"

"The extra five hundred thousand dollars," Ardath said. "That's a lot of zeros, isn't it? There's five before the decimal point and two after. Seven zeros. That is a terribly large amount of money."

"After the decimal point, you can have as many zeros as you want," Digger said. "You can make it an infinite number if you want."

Ardath Gillette thought about that for a moment. She said, "If the decimal is just a decimal, you can. But if it stands for the line of separation between dollars and cents, you can only have two zeros after it. Unless you want to get fractional."

"And who wants to get fractional?" Digger said. "I never thought of it in just that way."

"Most people don't. Then again most people don't think about anything. I suppose you insist on talking to my mother."

Digger nodded. "I guess so. I've come all this way; I might as well go through with it."

"Well, come on in," Ardath said. "I'll take you to her. She's playing with her trains."

Digger was sure he hadn't heard her right. Ardath stepped behind the big door and pulled it open wide for Digger to step through, then closed it behind him. He noticed that the left hand which she had kept behind her body while running him through her screening process was holding a paperback book.

Ardath walked off crisply, obviously expecting Digger to follow. They walked down a long hallway to the left. Digger heard what sounded like a train whistle and he guessed that he had heard Ardath correctly after all.

Ardath slid open large double doors at the end of the hallway and Digger heard the slightly constipated *whoop-whoop* of an electric train. He reached under his jacket and pushed the button turning on his tape recorder. Without evidence, no one would believe this—least of all, Walter Brackler. Somehow, Digger doubted that Brackler's last emissary had reported that Louise Gillette played with toy trains. Brackler was the kind of person who, had he been king, would kill the bearer of bad news.

Digger followed Ardath into the room. Obviously designed as a library, it was as large as his room at Gus LaGrande's Inn, and the walls were lined, floor to ceiling, with bookshelves packed full with books, magazines, paperbacks, newspapers. While the room had once been a library, almost every available inch of floor space was taken up now by an electric train layout. Track ran all around the floor. Portions of other track rose from the floor on steel supports until they were six feet high. Digger looked around and saw a section of track against one wall, as close to the ceiling as it could be and still allow the trains to fit in the narrow opening.

But there was something odd about the train layout, and Digger looked at it hard to figure out what it was. Then he realized what it was. Train layouts generally included a lot of bucolic towns, pastoral scenes, plastic cows grazing on Astroturf grass, ceramic farmers leaning on styrofoam plows and watching the trains passing by. Not this train set. There were no farms or pastoral scenes. There were elevated platforms with garbage overflowing trash baskets, with little two-inch-high people in business suits standing cheek by jowl with people in cutoff jeans who wore bandannas around their heads. He saw a train steaming by at waist level right in front of him. There was no traditional toy engine pulling a string of cars. Instead, the train was led by one car identical to the string of cars that followed it, little oval windows making them look like something used to transport prisoners. And on the outside of each car every available square inch of space was covered with brightly colored graffiti. Digger recognized RICO 177. He saw REMO

LIVES before the train whisked past him and into a tunnel constructed through the base of a building. In the window of the last car, he saw the letters AA.

Mrs. Gillette's train set was a replica of the New York City subway system, complete to graffiti, people packed into cars, and yes... Digger looked down at one of the platforms. Behind a turnstile was a replica of a city subway token booth and a two-inch-high armed robber was splashing gasoline on it. In his free hand he held a lighted match. Inside the booth, the woman token clerk was screaming silently, her face distorted in terror. Past the turnstiles, in a darkened corner of the miniature subway platform, Digger saw a man being mugged by four denim-jacketed toughs. Another ceramic figure urinated against a wall.

Digger looked around for the architect of all this madness.

To the left, he saw the back of a figure, hunched over a control board, shoulders scroonched up in a parody of a mad scientist chortling over some particularly evil arrangement of test tubes. The figure wore a red-and-white vertical-striped silk shirt. A railroader's blue-and-white cap sat atop its head, and from under the cap stray tendrils of dark hair twisted down onto the neck.

Digger glanced at Ardath, who was staring at him coolly.

"Mrs. Gillette?" he called out, but the sound of his voice was drowned out by the cacophony of trains whooping around the room, huffing out their asthmatic whistles.

Ardath gave him a look of great pity, then walked to a section of track that almost reached her shoulders and flicked a switch. The sounds of the trains diminished and died as everything rolled to a stop.

Digger saw the person at the control panel pressing buttons furiously, presumably wondering what act of God had halted the entire New York City subway system.

"Mother," Ardath called out, her voice echoing in the high-ceilinged room.

The train engineer turned. Digger would not have been surprised to see a twisted Phantom-of-the-Opera leer on a lipless face, with eyes sunken deep into sockets and a Singer sewing machine scar stitched neatly down one cheek.

What he got instead was a beautiful brunette woman. Digger

remembered that she would be in her mid-to late-thirties, but this woman could have been only twenty-one. Her lightly tanned skin was smooth and wrinkle-free. Her eyes were, like Ardath's, a brilliant green and there was a quizzical look in them, as if she detected humor where no one else could see it. Her lips were lightly glossed with a beige-colored lipstick. Long natural lashes made her large eyes seem even larger, and they appeared somehow luminous, as if a tiny pair of spotlights were shining on them from somewhere in the room.

"Mother," Ardath repeated, "this is Mr. Julian Burroughs. He's from the insurance company."

"I see," Mrs. Gillette said. Her face frosted over but was still without wrinkles. She said to Ardath, "Suppose you leave us, dear. I imagine we'll be talking business."

"Don't sign anything," Ardath said.

"I won't, dear. Run along now."

Ardath nodded, but as she turned and walked past Digger, she looked up at him and shrugged, a shrug that contained two million years of hurt and resentment and said, "See, treated like a juvenile again." She closed the sliding doors behind her as she left the train room.

"I'm sorry," Louise Gillette said. "Your name was…"

"Julian Burroughs, Mrs. Gillette. I'm with Brokers Surety Life Insurance."

"I know the name of your company, Mr. Burroughs," she said. "It seems my life is doomed to be one of never-ending correspondence and conference with you people."

"Not we people," Digger said. "I think this whole thing is stupid. I think we ought to give you the five hundred grand, call it quits and let you get on with rebuilding the New York subway system."

"Good. Have you brought a check?"

"No. They wouldn't trust me with that much money. Actually, they wouldn't trust me with the price of a pack of cigarettes."

"It's funny, you don't look like a corporate vice-president," she said.

"Perish forbid," Digger said. "Actually, I'm kind of an investigator for Br—for that insurance company whose name you know so well."

"And just what is it you're investigating?" Louise Gillette asked.

"I'll tell it to you the way it was told to me," Digger said.

"I wish you would."

"Go up there and find out what it takes to convince this crazy broad to take an extra half a million. I was also told that your elevator doesn't go to the top floor."

She studied him with a measured gaze, then rose from her seat in front of the control panel and walked toward him, stopping only when there was a thin section of track separating them.

"That still doesn't explain why they sent you. You're an investigator."

"But I am fabled for my tact and diplomacy," Digger said. "It's why they keep me around."

"I don't think you're going to last long enough to collect your pension," she said. "Tell me why you think wanting to protect my husband's reputation makes me a crazy broad."

"You misunderstand, Mrs. Gillette. I didn't say you were a crazy broad. My boss, Walter Brackler, complain to him—I'll give you his home address and phone number—*he* said you were a crazy broad. I came out here because I needed an excuse to drive to Pennsylvania and see my girl friend."

She was silent for a moment, and Digger said, "Mrs. Gillette, let's get it straight. I'm sort of a consultant for Old Benevolent and Saintly. I solve problems for them. They asked me to try to solve this problem concerning your insurance payment. I frankly don't give a rat's ass whether you take the million or the half million or if you send them money. It's all the same to me. I came out here for personal reasons. But I'm the company's last best hope, and yours, too, I suspect. After me, it goes to the legal department and then it'll be in court for a hundred and fifty years until senility lowers Ardath's IQ to five hundred and fifty and you finally get your first wrinkle. But just to touch the bases and tell them I tried, I did want to see you and find out exactly what were your reasons for refusing the extra five hundred thousand. It seems like kind of a large commitment to an arbitrary principle."

The woman folded her arms for a moment. "Principles are worth nothing unless they are arbitrary," she said. "If it's flexible, it's not a principle, it's a sometime rule. But if you're going to be the last of the pests, I don't mind talking to you. At least you're honest and you're not smiling all the time like the last insipid cretin they sent to see me. Can I get you a drink?"

"I thought you'd never ask. I always get thirsty in train stations. Vodka."

"Soda? Tonic? Ice?"

"Ice. Hold the adulterants."

"Okay. And thank you for the compliment about the wrinkles."

She lifted the section of track that had been separating them, much like a bartender getting out from behind the bar. He noticed that all the sections of track were hinged and could be opened the same way. Louise Gillette closed the track behind her and walked to a small walnut side-bar built into the base of the bookshelves. She poured his drink, but instead of handing it to him, she put it atop a railroad car and hit a switch. He watched his drink make a slow run around the room before coming to a stop on the section of track in front of him.

"Do you really think that's cute?" Digger asked as he picked up his drink and sipped it.

She did not turn until she had finished making her own drink, a Bloody Mary.

"Just a habit," she said.

"How does a woman get to be a model-train nut, if you'll pardon the turn of phrase?"

"Your maiden name is Louise Randisi. Your father's name was Louis and he wanted a boy. When you were born, he names you Louise and treats you like a boy. You get your first set of trains when you're four years old. You're a genius but your immigrant Italian family doesn't understand from geniuses. You study on your own and learn what you can but you play with trains. You get good enough to design them for toy manufacturers. Answer your question?"

"And you play with them in your spare moments?"

"I get paid for *playing* with them, as you put it, Mr. Burroughs. I've got a half-dozen patents on new computerized controls, new tracking mix systems. I've designed electronic computer games that can be played with model railroads. This subway design should be one of the big hits of next season. And besides, I'm from New York and I miss the subways. I miss everything, being up here in Belton."

"Go back to New York. You can afford it."

"I intend to," she said. She walked back, slid under a section of track and stood behind it as if it were a wall, sipping her red drink. "I'm going back, but I'm waiting till the end of the school year. It's important that Ardath not be uprooted unnecessarily. Her friends are here. She'll be better able to handle separation during the summer vacation than right now. She's already had quite enough shocks this year."

Digger resisted saying, so did your electrocuted husband. He merely nodded.

"I still don't understand why your company sent an investigator here," she said.

"I was all they had left," Digger said. "I'm the burned rice on the bottom of the pot."

"So I'm reduced to dealing with scrapings, all because I refuse to take their extra half million."

"Something like that. Tell me, don't you need the money? Would you mind taking off that railroad cap? I feel like I'm on the Wabash Cannonball and you're going to ask me for my ticket."

She took off the hat with a small smile. Piles of black curls tumbled about her face. She had been pretty before. Now she was beautiful, Digger thought.

"Better?" she asked.

"Immeasurably."

"You asked me if I don't need your company's money. No, I don't. I make a great deal more as a designer than my husband did in electronics."

"Why don't you think he died in an accident?" Digger asked.

"Because it's impossible. Vern was a genius of the highest order, an absolute whiz in his field. His dying in an electrical accident makes him sound like a fool. He was no fool. I can only believe that he died of a heart attack or some medical reason."

"Was his health poor?" Digger asked.

"Of course not. When I decided to marry, I carefully picked a man who was the picture of health. Vern was tall, perfectly formed. He had been an athlete in college. He kept himself in the best of shape. That's his photograph over there."

She pointed to a section of the bookcase where a photo stood inside a simple gold frame. Digger walked over to look at it. Vernon Gillette was handsome, all right. The picture had been taken in college, because Digger recognized the distinctive football uniform of the UCLA Bruins. Gillette was tall and lean and his face was open and honest, with handsome, regular features. He would not have been out of place playing lifeguard on a Malibu beach.

"Then how a heart attack? It's not logical."

"Believe me, it's a great deal more likely and logical than an accident," she said stubbornly. "Refill that drink?"

"No," Digger said. "Stay there. I'll do it myself. Are you ready for another?"

"No. I have one drink every two days. This is it until the day after tomorrow. Help yourself."

"That's my rule too," Digger said. "This drink is for Wednesday, March sixteenth, in the year 2654."

As Digger poured his drink, she said, "My husband couldn't have died in the type of accident your company has determined."

"My company didn't make that determination, Mrs. Gillette. The police did." He looked through the sparse liquor supply for Finlandia but settled instead for cheap American vodka with a pseudo-Russian name.

"Nevertheless, your company is attempting to pay on the basis of that assumption, and I cannot allow it."

"Why not?" Digger asked. "Take the goddamn money and run. What difference does it make?"

"First of all, I don't need the money. Secondly, it involves Vern's reputation. I think it is important for Ardath not to grow up believing her father was a fool."

"Do you think it matters to her?" Digger asked. He turned with his drink in his hand, leaned on the bar and looked at the woman who was diddling one of the small model subway cars with her finger, as if she had found a speck of real dirt hidden under the carefully designed graffiti.

"She would probably say no, but I have to be the best judge of that. I think someday it might. Do you have children, Mr. Burroughs?"

"Yes."

"Then I'm surprised you don't understand."

"You wouldn't be if you saw What's-his-name and the girl," Digger said. "But why a heart attack?"

"Why not?" she said.

"Maybe it was something else," he said.

"He was in perfect health," she said.

"That ought to preclude heart attacks too."

"Mr. Burroughs, all I want from your company is my five hundred thousand dollars. Not some ill-formed medical judgment."

"All right, I'll tell them that," Digger said. And, he thought, I'll play the tape recording, certifying that you are a full-blown, dyed-in-the-wool crazy. "Will you sign a document to that effect, freeing the company from any future legal liability?"

"Yes. I tried to tell the other one that. The one who kept smiling."

"Okay." Digger drained his vodka. "I can find my own way out."

"Thank you," she said. Digger replaced his glass on the bar. When he turned back, she had already put her railroad cap back on and was hunched over the control panel. As he opened the room's double doors, he heard the whooping of train whistles as the model railroad started up behind him.

Walking down the hallway, he passed an open door and glanced inside. Ardath was sitting in an armchair, a leg flung casually over the chair's arm, reading from a book. Digger leaned into the doorway.

"So long, Ardath."

She looked up. "Oh, so long," she said. She stood up and said soberly, "Couldn't convince her, could you?"

"No."

"She's really quite truculent about some things."

"Yes, she is. What are you reading?"

"Just a book," she said. She stuck it into her pocket and walked with Digger toward the front door.

"Do you think your father died of a heart attack?" Digger asked. He put his big hand on her thin little shoulder.

"Do you really want to know?" she asked.

"Yes."

"No, I don't," Ardath said.

"You agree with the police? An accident, right?"

"No. Daddy was too smart to have an accident," she said.

"What, then?"

"You don't really want to know," Ardath said. "I'm going to tell you and you're going to say, what do you know, you're just a kid, and you'll dismiss it all."

"Honest, I won't say that," Digger said.

"Promise?"

"Yes. And an insurance man's promise is as eternal as the sands of the desert," Digger said.

"I think he was murdered," she said.

"What?"

"There you go," she said. "You're starting. Next thing, you're going to say, 'You're just a kid, what do you know?'"

"No, I'm not. Why do you think he was murdered?"

"I think a lot of people are murdered and no one ever knows its murder," she said.

"I heard there was a lot of it going around," Digger said. Ardath held the door open for him, but before going through it, Digger reached behind the little girl and plucked the book from her jeans.

It had a garish red-and-white cover, the white serving as a backdrop for the big globs of blood that spelled out the title: *The Palindrome Murders* by a writer Digger had never heard of.

"You read a lot of these?" Digger said, giving her back the book and feeling guilty about intruding on her life, almost as if he had been caught peeking into her bedroom.

"Yes, Mr. Burroughs," she said, solemn and hurt. "I read a lot of mysteries because they are always tidy. Murders are always known to be murders and murderers are always captured or done away with. But that has nothing to do with my feeling about my father's death."

"All right. If he was murdered, who murdered him?"

"I was hoping you might find out." She smiled sheepishly. "I listened for a while at the door. I know you're an investigator."

"I'll be seeing you around, Ardath," he said as he left.

Chapter Three

Digger aimed his car down toward Belton's bowl. It was very simple. He had driven straight up on the main street until he had found Gillette's house. All he had to do to get back was to turn around and go straight down in the direction he had come from.

He got lost.

Since he always got lost driving around in a car, this didn't bother him. Nor did the fact that somehow he wound up on a back highway which seemed not to be a part of Belton at all, because it was level and flat, not sloping the way it should have been if he were still anywhere inside the bowl.

What did bother him was that it was past lunchtime and he had not yet seen a tavern on this road.

And another thing that bothered him was that he was being followed.

He had spotted the red pickup truck about ten minutes into his confused rambling and had slowed down to let it pass, but it slowed down too. Then he speeded up to get away from it and it speeded up too. At first he had thought it was some idiot driver who wanted his truck to be friends with a car with New York license plates, but when he made a couple of left and right turns, trying desperately to find a cocktail lounge or a bar, the truck stayed with him and Digger knew he was being tailed.

The truck was still following him when he saw a tavern up ahead on the left side of the main road. Carefully, because he did not want his car to be buggered by some klutzy pickup truck, he put on his left directional, slowed down and pulled into the tavern's parking lot.

His was the only car but there were four other vehicles, all pickup trucks. As he pulled into a parking spot, he saw the red truck drive past and keep going. For a moment he thought that maybe he had been wrong; maybe he wasn't being followed. Yes, of course. And maybe he didn't drink too much either.

He whistled softly to himself as he walked toward the entrance. A garish neon sign proclaimed it as Eddie's. Bars like that, he thought, were always named by their owner after their owner. Every man wanted to be immortalized. Twenty years from now, when Eddie was dead from erysipelas, the scientists would come by and cart Eddie's away, termite-infested board by termite-infested board, and reassemble it in the Smithsonian Institute as a particularly grisly example of *Roadhouse Americanus*, and Eddie would live forever in the hearts and minds of his fellow countrymen.

He glanced at the parking lot again and began to sing, "I'll be down to get you in my pickup, honey. Better be ready when the big hand's on six and the little hand's between eight and nine."

The owners of the pickup fleet outside were all sitting at the bar when Digger entered. All four of them turned to look at him, staring at him with the rudeness commonly practiced on strangers by people who are in their hometowns. Digger could have walked into a roadhouse in Alabama and gotten exactly the same looks from four Alabama chain-saw mechanics as he did from these four Pennsylvania gorillas. The look was a curious mixture of: Who Are You? What Are You Doing Here? If You're Looking for Trouble, Sucker, You Found It. Are You Some Communist Come to Steal Our Homes and Land? And, No, I Gave at the Office.

Digger glanced at the four men impassively and wished that he was wearing a Nehru outfit, complete with pantaloons and silken leg wraps, because that would really have made their day.

As soon as he had sat down at a table near the large front window of Eddie's, a waitress swooped down on him.

Behind her, Digger could see the four men, identical in their plaid shirts and jeans, turn back to the television, which was roaring a baseball game at the world. They looked, he thought, like a gang bang waiting to happen.

And the waitress looked like the object of their affections.

She was stuffed into a white uniform whose three top buttons were opened, showing rounded mounds of cleavage that looked curiously to Digger like a pair of buttocks. The face above the chest was pretty but vacant. The woman's blue eyes had been outlined with pencil in a cobalt blue color. Her hair was platinumed and piled up around her head. There seemed to be so much hair spray on it that it didn't even shiver when she walked or when she leaned over Digger's table, inviting him to get lost in her chest, as she slapped a knife, fork and paper napkin on the formica table in front of him.

"Afternoon," she said. "Want a menu?"

"No thanks, Dolly. I'll just have a vodka on the rocks."

"How'd you know my name was Dolly?"

"Gee, I don't know. You just kind of reminded me of somebody named Dolly, I guess."

She smiled warmly. "Dolly Parton," she said.

"That's right."

"Everybody says I look like Dolly Parton. I don't know. It must be the blond hair or something."

"A lot of people have blond hair," Digger said. "I think it's the 'something.'"

"You're not from around here, are you?" she said, and Digger thought, obviously not, because I've been talking to you for twenty seconds already and I haven't once mentioned my pickup truck or my new hand-tooled leather boots.

"No," he said. "Just passing through."

"Too bad. You might like Belton."

"The only thing I like about Belton is standing right in front of me," Digger said.

"Well, thank you, sir," she said. "I love all you smooth-talking travelers who wander in here and try to turn a girl's head."

"You been living in Belton long?" Digger asked.

"Long enough."

"You like living in a town without air?" he asked.

"The smoke? It's not that bad," she said. "You kinda get used to it."

"If you don't, you'd better, right?" Digger said. "The Beltons are pretty important people, I guess."

"You said it. Old Lucius, he's like the town daddy, and we're his children."

It sounded to Digger as if she were describing God.

"What's he like?"

"Who?"

"Town daddy Lucius."

"I ain't never met him," she said, as if the question were absurd. "But he's gotta be all right. I mean, he's over seventy if he's a day and he's got a wife who probably ain't even thirty yet. That takes a man, doesn't it?"

"Or a lot of money," Digger said.

"I guess you're right," she said with a laugh that seemed surprisingly sincere. "What's your name anyway, stranger?"

"Clem," said Digger. "Clem Barff. That's with two *F*s. *F* as in fellatio."

"I'll be sure to remember that. Vodka rocks, you said?"

"Make it a double," Digger said.

There was a hawk-nosed man behind the bar who engaged Dolly in rapid conversation when she came back behind the bar. The four customers leaned forward on their stools to listen. Digger couldn't hear what they were saying over the roar of the television, but he knew they were talking about him and he didn't care.

He glanced through the window and saw the red pickup truck backing into a parking spot that faced the door of Eddie's. The afternoon sun kicked up a glare from the windshield and Digger could not see the driver's face.

Dolly returned with his drink, a regular-sized beer glass filled with ice cubes and vodka.

"Sorry," she said. "No rocks glasses. All we do here is shots and beers usually."

"No problem. As long as it doesn't leak. You see that red pickup out there?"

He nodded toward the parking lot and Dolly leaned over him to look, threatening to engulf him in her chest. He thought if her bra straps ever broke, she might just plunge through the floor and into the cellar.

"Yeah," she said.

"You know who it is?" Digger said.

"No. He ain't one of our regulars 'cause I know all their trucks."

"I bet you do. Would you do me a favor?"

"I'll try," she said.

"Bring me back a bottle of beer."

"Something wrong with your vodka?"

"No, no, it's fine. Please. A bottle of beer."

"Okay."

She went back to the bar and engaged in more whispered conversation while Digger dragged one of his business cards from his wallet. The card just listed his name and the name of Brokers Surety Life Insurance Company.

On the back of it, Digger wrote, "If you're going to wait, don't wait dry."

Digger also took a five-dollar bill from his wallet.

When Dolly came back, Digger slipped the five into her hand.

"That's for you. Would you take this beer out to the guy in the red pickup truck?"

"Huh?"

"Give the beer to the guy in the truck. And give him this card too."

"Oh," she said.

"He's waiting for me," Digger said.

"Okay." She looked at the card. "Who's this? Julian Burroughs."

Digger shrugged. "I don't know. Some insurance salesman who gave me his card. I save junk like that."

She nodded, a very knowing nod. Digger noticed that she had a beauty mark near the left corner of her mouth, and he wondered who first decided that moles on the face would be called beauty marks if the owner was pretty. And what was the cutoff age when young women's beauty marks became old crones' moles?

Dolly took the bottle of beer outside and sashayed across the parking lot to the red pickup. She walked, hip-swinging suggestively in almost a parody of sexual invitation. She went to the driver's side of the pickup, said a few words to the driver and handed the bottle into the truck. Then she came back to the bar, and a few moments later the driver got out of the truck and walked toward the bar too.

Digger didn't think you could tell anything about people from their faces. That was his intellectual position, although his instincts told him he would rather be with smiling, smooth-faced people than with some leering ape with a face that looked like a testing range for buckshot. Still, as he watched the young man following Dolly toward the door of the roadhouse, he felt he was an unlikely candidate to be tailing someone. The man was tall and lean with a broad forehead, neatly trimmed hair and features that were regular and as uninteresting as a television test pattern. He looked vaguely like a high school English teacher, much beloved by his students, about whom the worst that one could imagine would be that he had an envelope of *fin-de-stècle* French postcards hidden behind his t-shirts in his dresser drawer. Digger turned on his tape recorder.

Inside the roadhouse, Dolly nodded the man toward Digger's table, and he came over and slid onto the bench opposite Digger's. He looked sheepish.

"Thanks for the drink," he said.

"Least I could do. Tailing somebody's hard work."

"I thought I was doing pretty well too," the man said glumly.

"Take my word for it, you weren't," Digger said. "So who are you and what do you want with me?" Digger glanced over toward the bar, but Eddie and the four morons were engrossed in the baseball game. Dolly was washing glasses. No one was paying attention to Digger and this man.

The man was holding Digger's card and he looked at it again.

"Julian Burroughs?"

"That's right. Who are you?"

"Cody Lord. Vernon Gillette was my friend."

"So what? What cause does that give you to follow me?"

"None, I guess," Lord said. "I was just wondering who you were and what you wanted."

"You always follow insurance men?" Digger asked. He looked toward the bar, caught Dolly's eye and pointed to his glass for another drink. She smiled and nodded.

"No," Lord said. "I heard you at Louise's and she told me you were an investigator. You a detective?"

"To a detective, I'm not a detective. To somebody who follows as badly as you do, I'm a detective," Digger said. "Why?"

"I know what you told Louise, that you were up here to try to get her to take the money…" He looked up at Digger as if hoping to be interrupted. Digger was silent. "...but you told her you were an investigator and I thought you might be here for more than that."

"Like what?"

"Like looking into the cause of Vern's death," Lord said.

"Why should I do that?"

"I think—"

"Hold it," Digger said, looking up as Dolly approached their table. With a large smile, she set a drink down in front of Digger, picked up his empty glass, dumped his ashtray of dead cigarettes into a paper napkin, hovered as much as she could without being too obvious, then vibrated away.

"You were saying?"

"I think Vern was killed."

"Why?" Digger asked.

"I don't know."

"That's a lot to go on," Digger said in disgust. He saw that Lord looked pained and he said, "Why don't you start slow and kind of build up to it?"

"All right. Vern was my friend. We worked together at Belton and Sons. I was with him up at the cabin where he died. We were up there to go deer hunting for the weekend, but that first night I couldn't stay and I had to leave. He stayed up there alone. I was the one who found him when I came back the next day. I couldn't believe that he was dead. I still can't believe it."

"Why'd you go home?" Digger asked.

"What?"

"You said you couldn't stay that night. Why not?"

Lord hesitated, then shrugged. "I had some family things I had to do. Personal stuff."

Digger let it pass.

"Why do you think it was a murder?"

"I got up there and I found Vern was dead but...I don't know... there was somebody else there. I don't know how I know. Does that make any sense?"

"About as much as I've come to expect of you," Digger said. "Why do you think there was somebody there? Footprints? Cigarette butts in the ashtray? Beds slept in? What?"

There was a slow growing light shining behind Cody Lord's eyes. "You know I never thought of that."

"Share it with me now. Enrich both our lives."

"Both beds were mussed," Lord said. "And they were made when I left and I didn't sleep there. Maybe that's what made me think somebody was there."

"What size beds were they?"

"Huh? Oh, little beds. Almost like army cots." He looked off into space. "Yeah, both of them were unmade. Maybe it kind of registered but didn't really, if you know what I mean."

"Yeah. I know what you mean without knowing what you mean," Digger said. "His wife said he was too smart to stick his finger in a socket or whatever he's supposed to have done."

"She's right. Vern was smart and I can't figure him getting killed in an accident that way, but accidents happen to everybody. I guess it was the slept-in bed."

"What about a heart attack? That's what his wife thinks."

"He had the physical condition of a kid. He never had anything wrong with his heart. Anybody can have a heart attack, I guess, but I wouldn't figure he did."

"All right. Who'd want to kill him?" Digger asked.

"I don't know."

"Somebody at work? Maybe he was stepping on somebody's toes?"

"I don't think so. Everybody liked Vern," Lord said.

"Maybe somebody was going south with company money and Gillette found out about it."

"He would have told me," Lord said. "He was my friend."

"Okay, then. Tell me about Gillette. What women was he fooling around with?"

"What?"

"You heard me," Digger said.

"Mr. Burroughs, I don't think—"

Digger interrupted, "That's exactly right. You *don't* think. Try it though. Maybe you'll like it. Now you say the second bed was slept in and it wasn't by you. So maybe he had company. Maybe a forest ranger with frostbitten toes stopped in to spend the night. Maybe Smokey the Bear showed up and needed a room after spending a busy day harassing people about their cigarette butts. Or maybe some broad showed up to play house. That's not all the possibilities, not by a long shot, but out of those three I like the last one best. What woman or women was he involved with?"

"I don't know anything about that," Lord said. Digger knew he was lying by the way he looked away as soon as he finished the sentence.

"When did you guys go up to the cabin?"

"Last deer season," Lord said.

"What day of the week?"

"Saturday," Lord said. "We went up Saturday morning."

"And you found his body Sunday morning?"

"That's right."

"Did he know you were going to go home Saturday night?"

"I don't follow you," Lord said.

"What do you do for a living?" Digger asked.

"I'm in the quality-control department at Belton and Sons."

"Christ, no wonder nothing works in America anymore. Did Gillette know you were going home Saturday night?"

"Yes. I guess so. I told him I'd have to."

"When did you tell him?"

"I guess it was the day before," Lord said.

"Did you go up there in your pickup?"

"Yes."

"So he was up there Saturday night without a car?" Digger said. Lord nodded.

"Okay," Digger said and turned his attention back to his drink.

"What does that mean, okay?"

"It just means thank you for your time and I don't want to hold you up any longer. There must be other people you have to follow."

"You don't believe me, do you?"

"It's not belief," Digger said. "It's conviction. Sure, I think you really believe that somebody killed Gillette. But you haven't given me one reason that would convince me. The mussed-up bed probably belonged to a girl friend who drove up, and you're lying to me about not knowing who she was. What time did you get up there Sunday morning?"

"I don't know. Around eleven," Lord said.

"How long had he been dead?"

"How would I know?"

"Well, if the corpse was still bleeding, you'd know it was pretty recent. Try this. Was he warm? Most living people and recently dead people are warm. Except maybe in Belton, PA."

"I don't think I like you, Mr. Burroughs."

"That's fine. I don't much like myself. I'm only able to go on because I like other people a lot less. Including you."

"All right," Lord said. He slid down the bench toward the end of the table, as if getting ready to leave. "There was almost an accident, Mr. Burroughs."

"What kind of an accident?"

"The brakes failed on Vern's car, right after he had a brake job. He almost got killed."

"Maybe a coincidence and maybe a bad garage mechanic," Digger said.

"And maybe somebody trying to kill him," Lord said. "Vern told me once that he was going to make...what'd he call it...a big score."

"What was he talking about?"

"I don't know," Lord said. "He wouldn't tell me."

"I don't blame him," Digger said. "Did Mrs. Gillette know about his near accident that maybe wasn't an accident?"

"I don't think Vern wanted to worry her," Lord said.

"Did you ever tell her how you feel? That it was murder?"

"Yes. I thought she ought to know."

"What'd she think?" Digger asked.

"She said I was crazy."

"She would recognize the symptoms," Digger said. "Did you tell the police?"

"You can't tell them anything," Cody Lord said. "They had accidental death written in their book before they even got to the cabin."

"Let me ask you something else," Digger said. "When you told Mrs. Gillette about your suspicions, could Ardath have overheard you?"

"I don't know. She was in the house, I guess. She might have."

Digger said, "Lord, if I were to do something, what would you want me to do?"

"I don't know. I thought, well, you being a detective, maybe you could find out what really happened to Vern."

"Sorry, pal. I just don't see anything yet to find out."

"Sorry to have wasted your time," Lord said stiffly. He got up from the bench.

"I'm at Gus's LaGrande Inn," Digger said. "Anytime you feel like telling me the whole truth, you can reach me there."

The thin sandy-haired man looked at Digger for a moment, as if trying to decide whether to say something or not. Instead, he just nodded and walked toward the door. Digger noticed that he had not taken even a sip from his beer.

Dolly approached the table.

"Would you like another drink?" She hesitated a moment, then added, "Clem. Traveling does make a soul thirsty."

"Come on," Digger said. "You know my name's not Clem. You read my card. And I know your IQ is higher than your bust size, so you can get off the Mammy Yokum routine and save it for the locals."

"Fair enough," she said. "It gets to be a pain in the ass after a while anyway," she said.

"Can you sit down and join me for a drink?"

"Afraid not. Eddie doesn't like it if I drink with customers during working hours. They might get the wrong idea."

"How about not during working hours?"

"Eddie employs me. He doesn't own me," she said.

"Anybody own you?"

"A lot of people, but it's too complicated to tell you about now. Maybe sometime when we've got more time."

"Well, if your path ever takes you to the bar in Gus's LaGrande Inn, you'll find me there."

"I'll keep it in mind. What are you in town for?"

"Insurance on a guy named Gillette," Digger said. "Your name's not really Dolly, is it?"

"Sorry, that part's authentic. It's Dolly," she said.

"Well," Digger said and smiled at her, "hello, Dolly."

"Hi, Koko."

"Oh, hello, Digger. How goes the insurance business in Belton?"

"Stupid," he said. "I'm trying to convince some woman to take an extra half a million dollars of our company money. He died in an accident. She thinks he had a heart attack. His daughter thinks he was murdered. It's all very strange. How is it with you?"

"I'm not sure yet."

"What's wrong?" Digger asked.

"My sister needs a couple more tests. We won't know for a while about that operation."

"I should be there with you in your moment of need."

"No, Digger, not now."

"Why not?"

"It's my mother. She doesn't deal with pressure all that well and she's a wreck. I've got to nursemaid her every minute."

"I'll come out there and hold her hand," Digger said.

"The last time you got together with her in Las Vegas, you got her all liquored up, and you know she's like me, she can't drink. Then you bought her three cameras so she'd look like all the other Japanese in Las Vegas. I've never forgiven you for that."

"I won't do it this time. She's already got her three cameras out of me."

"No, Dig. We should know something soon. Tell me about your day."

"Terrific. I met a lunatic, and a genius, and a guy who'd have to take a poll to decide if it was raining out, and a Dolly Parton look-alike."

"Knowing you, any one of those four things could keep you busy for another day anyway," Koko said.

"I don't want to be busy with one of those things. I want to be busy with you. I thought we'd have a nice weekend. Koko's weekend."

"Digger, don't whine. You get very nasal and it's unbecoming. Did you convince that woman to take the money?"

"No. She rejected me too."

"Oh, poor baby. Nobody wants you."

"That's about the size of it," Digger said. "Here I am, looking out my window at this corral full of lalapaloozas, just yearning to be ridden, and I've got nobody to share it with." He glanced out his window. There was not a horse as far as the eye could see.

"I'd like to be there riding them," she said.

"I think I'm going back to Las Vegas soon," Digger said.

"Don't do that. I really want to be with you. Really. But I want everything here resolved first. Is that so hard to understand?"

"No, I understand very well," Digger said. "You don't want me around until things are right. Are they right when Hucko Slaphammer leaves town? Is that when they're going to be right?"

"Hugo Stockelbrinner," Koko corrected. "I can't believe this. Are you jealous of what I did when I was seventeen?"

"Yes," Digger said.

"Digger, go get drunk and call me tomorrow."

"That's two things I'll never forget," he said.

"What's that?" asked Koko.

"This and Pearl Harbor. Good-bye forever."

Digger hung up.

Chapter Four

Tape recording Number One and Only, 9:00 P.M., Thursday, Julian Burroughs in the matter of Tamiko Fanucci, roommate and worthless ingrate, and coincidentally in the matter of Louise Gillette, whose mind shall ever hereafter be known as The Wreck of the Old Ninety-Seven.

I hate it when I can't get over on women with my charm. Why doesn't Koko want me to come and see her in Emporium? What the hell kind of name for a town is Emporium anyway? Why won't she come here? What is she up to? Does she think it's any fun for me to be sitting in this room, drinking alone, looking up at the crimson dot in the chandelier that marks the very spot where Huckleberry Hackenberger deflowered her? This is fun? This is how she welcomes me to Pennsylvania?

What did I expect from a woman who's a blackjack dealer among other things? When I left my wife, Bruno, and the two kids, What's-his-name and the girl, a million years ago and I moved to Las Vegas, somebody told me never to trust a blackjack dealer. I should have listened.

Who told me that? Oh. Koko told me that. Well, she should know. If I ever open my apartment door again and find a beautiful young Eurasian naked in my hall, hysterical, never again will I invite her in. Never again will I go retrieve her clothes and purse. Oh, no. That was my mistake last time. Never again. The next time I will call the local vice squad and have her arrested for soliciting.

I'll perjure myself on the witness stand. I'll tell how she came scratching at my door. How when I wouldn't let her in, she slid her tongue under my door and licked the tips of my boots. How she made all kinds of vile propositions that I, as a decent, God-fearing American, would have nothing to do with. I'll nail her ass. Tamiko Fanucci, I sentence you to be taken from this place to another place and thence to a place where you shall be hanged by your gorgeous Oriental-Sicilian neck until you are dead, dead, dead.

And then, Koko, when I see them cut your body down, I'm going to go out and get drunk for a week in celebration.

On sake.

I will make a special occasion of it and drink your rotten warm Japanese rice wine and let you know just what I think of you. So how do you like them pomegranates?

What the hell is she doing in Emporium anyway? If I read that one Hucko Hangleglider has died of sexual exhaustion in Emporium, she is in deep and rich trouble.

Well, who cares? To hell with her.

And while I'm at it, to hell with Louise Gillette. There are two tapes in the master file. There will not be any more tapes in the master file.

But I did my master's bidding. I came to Belton, PA, to talk to Louise and convince her to take a million dollars.

Kwash will ask me. The head of the claims department will say to me, what kind of person is she, Digger, and I will say, Kwash, the lights are on but nobody is home. This woman is bat shit. She plays with trains. Not just trains but the New York subway system, complete with muggings and fire bombings.

But I think I impressed her. At least she said I was better than the last insipid cretin Old Benevolent and Saintly sent to see her. I think that's a compliment. She offered me a drink and I took it. I like taking drinks. This is because there has been so much pain in my life.

She doesn't believe her husband could have died in an electrical accident. What was it she said? She carefully picked a man who was perfectly formed. It sounds like she bought him at a livestock auction. Anyway, she doesn't want her daughter to think her father was a fool. If it were me and I had children who were not Cro-

Magnon, I would rather that they thought I left them a millionaire. I mean, how many fools leave their kids a million bucks?

Anyway, we blahed and blahed and she agreed to sign a document freeing the company from liability. She told the other cretin that too. The one with the teeth.

Ardath, the daughter, is another case. She is brilliant even if she does read mysteries. She says her father was murdered. I know where she got that idea from.

And that brings us to Tape Number Two.

This tape was recorded in Eddie's Roadside Sandwich Heaven between me and a Cody Lord who said he was Vernon Gillette's friend and who followed me from the Gillette house. Very clumsily.

He thinks Gillette was murdered too because a bed was slept in. This is where Ardath got her stupid idea from. Cody Lord was up there at the cabin with Gillette but went home for undisclosed personal reasons. I know that today's rejection by Koko has aged me but I am not yet senile. When Cody Lord told Gillette that he wouldn't be spending Saturday night at the cabin, Gillette arranged for somebody, presumably of the female persuasion, to sleep over. That seems reasonable and likely.

But I would still like to know why Cody Lord went home. And, come to think of it, I'd like to know how Cody Lord knew so much about my talk with Louise Gillette. First of all, how'd he get into the house and know I was there? That brass door knocker sounds like an ax smashing against the door. I guess so that Louise can hear it over the *huffa-huffa-puffa* of the subway system.

But I didn't hear anybody knock on the door when I was there. Does Cody Lord just walk into the Gillette house unannounced? Or does he sneak in the back?

I don't know. I'd like to know. Maybe I'll ask Ardath.

I also met Dolly today. Usually I censor these tapes so that Koko doesn't hear any of my worst moments, but this one I won't. I hope you hear this, you treacherous Nipponese. Dolly has a wonderful large set of pneumatics and she is available for the rolling-around-on. You hear that, Fanucci? She also acts like somebody without brain one, but the operative word there is "act." I suspect she sees what's going on and knows this town pretty well and if I had any intention at all of hanging around here, I could do a lot worse than talk to her and find out what is really going on in Belton. I'm sure that woman knows, and it would be pure research, chargeable to the company and about which you couldn't bitch.

Hah. Her bitch? While she's up there rutting with Hackney Hamburglar? Fat chance.

I may just hang out here another day. Not because of Koko, mind you, but because two people, at least one of them sane, have told me they think Gillette was murdered. Maybe I owe Frank Stevens a fast pass at that theory. Maybe I'll run into Dolly again. Maybe I'll have somebody take a picture of her and me dancing at the Saturday night stomping grounds and I'll have it blown up to wall-size and show it to Koko. I'll hang it over our bed in Las Vegas. That'll fix her rickshaw.

Time out. Expenses. Yesterday. Lunch on the road to Belton, nine dollars. Tips to waitresses and bellboys at Gus's LaGrande Inn—it's a fabulous place, Kwash, with a big staff—fifteen dollars. Dinner, twenty-one dollars including tip, and thirty-one dollars at the bar, interviewing town residents. Total, seventy-six dollars.

Today. Breakfast. Four dollars. Money to pump Cody Lord with booze, twenty-five dollars. He drinks like a fish. I'm going to eat dinner soon and I'll keep it under twenty dollars. So call it twenty dollars. Then I'm going to interview more townsfolk. I know more of them today than I did yesterday, so it'll cost more. Say forty dollars. Total, eighty-nine dollars. Two-day total, one hundred and sixty-five dollars.

I'm making this one sixty-six, Kwash, rounding it off to the next highest dollar because I'm tired of eating all the change.

Room, car rental and gas by credit card.

Chapter Five

Digger had once taken Koko and her mother to a fancy Italian restaurant just off the Las Vegas strip. The main dining room was coliseum-sized; there were a full dozen waiters and another dozen busboys hovering about; a piano-violin duo played softly, and the three of them were the only customers in the entire place.

Mrs. Fanucci had observed this silently, enjoyed her dinner, then leaned over to Digger and said, "This place doing no business."

"No, it isn't," he had agreed.

"Must be is a Mafia dry cleaner."

"What?"

"Must be is a Mafia dry cleaner," she repeated word for word.

Digger had looked to Koko in bewilderment.

"She means it's a Mafia laundry. Where they wash dirty money," Koko explained.

"Exactly," Mrs. Fanucci said. "Is washing money."

She then turned to Koko and said "Tamiko" and followed it with a soft babble of Japanese.

"What'd she say?" Digger asked.

"She wanted to know why anybody wanted to wash money."

"Tell her that's why they call it filthy lucre," Digger had said.

He had occasion to think about that as he sat alone in the barroom of Gus's LaGrande Inn. All those dining rooms, all the bar space, all the acreage. What paid for it? Not one solitary drinker, even if he was of Digger's world-class category. Not eight guest rooms at thirty-five dollars a night. Not even a reasonably good lunch and dinner trade. Digger suspected that young Gus LaGrande's books might not bear too much inspection.

It was eleven o'clock and Digger had been drinking for almost two hours. Gus had mixed up a few rounds of drinks for his late-dinner trade, but since that time had spent most of his time going through stacks of bills. He seemed to break the large stack into smaller stacks, then go through the smaller stacks to make substacks. And when he was done, and the large pile of bills was in twelve different little piles, he put them all together again and started over.

A young woman wearing a loose fluffy sweater came into the bar and sat across from Digger. In the dim light, Digger could see little more than the woman's wavy brown hair and her smooth unlined face. It was a pretty, warm face.

Gus stopped in front of the woman. Digger heard them mumble, then watched Gus mix her a Scotch and soda. Gus walked up to Digger.

"Lady says she'd like to buy you a drink. Says she knows you."

Digger looked past him at the woman, who met his eyes briefly, then glanced down at her drink.

"I think she's mistaken," Digger said aloud. "I never forget a beautiful woman and I don't know her. But I'll drink. Move me around the bar."

Digger sat on the stool next to the woman, who still did not look up from her drink. Gus put his vodka glass in front of him.

"Cheers," Digger said, holding his glass up to click with the woman's. "Where do we know each other from?"

The woman looked up and smiled at him. "Why how quickly you forget, Mr. Barff. With two *f*'s. As in fellatio."

Digger looked at her carefully, then smiled back.

"All right, Dolly," he said. "You win. You had me going. I didn't recognize you without that haymow on your head."

"Don't forget the beauty mark on my lip. That's gone too," she said.

"The mark's gone. The beauty stays," Digger said.

"How gallant."

"I haven't even started yet. Now I know why you were wearing that sweater. In something tight, I'd know you anywhere."

"Something like that," she agreed.

"I'm glad you found me. I might have spent the whole night driving the streets of Belton, looking for a house with a platinum wig drying in the window."

"That's nice," she said, "but somehow I get the idea that you probably would have just spent the rest of the night sitting here getting ripped."

"Only problem drinkers prefer to drink alone," Digger said.

"You're not a problem drinker?"

"It's never given *me* any problem," Digger said. "Well, sometimes it does. Like I used to drink Russian vodka and then I got to hate the Russians, so I stopped drinking their vodka. That was a problem. It would have been a bigger problem if only the French made vodka besides the Russians, 'cause I hate the French too. Fortunately, though, everybody makes vodka. I drink vodka from Finland. But the Japanese make vodka and so do the Red Chinese. I haven't forgiven them for Laos and Cambodia yet, though, so I won't drink their vodka either. Polish vodka either."

"You're rapidly running out of world," she said.

"Don't worry. The Third World's going to start making vodka soon. They're going to make it out of crocodile sweat. That'll give me another thirty countries to hate."

"You're a very complicated man."

"You're the second beautiful female to tell me that today."

"Oh?"

"The other one was eight years old."

"Is that what you're doing up here? Visiting family? It's Julian, isn't it?"

"Julian Burroughs. But everybody calls me Digger. You can call me Dig. That's special, for good friends."

"Thank you," she said. "You were telling me what you were doing up here?"

"No, actually I wasn't, or at least I hadn't started to yet, and I was making up my mind whether to tell you the truth or to lie."

"Why would you lie?" she asked.

"The truth is a dull and colorless thing. And I'm a very imaginative liar."

"Try the truth for size," she said. "Dig," she added.

Digger noticed that Gus LaGrande was back at the end of the bar, repiling his bills. One thing had to be said about the man—he didn't intrude on customers' musings or conversations.

"All right. I work for an insurance company. I came to town to try to talk some woman into taking some of our money."

"Were you successful?"

"No. She turned me down cold."

"Obviously, you were talking to the wrong woman," Dolly said. "If you wanted me to take some of your company's money, I'd be glad to."

"I wish I had known that before I got my company committed to this other woman," Digger said.

"Why won't she take your money? That doesn't make any sense. Did she have a death in the family?"

"Yes. And we think it's an accident and want to pay her double indemnity and she says it wasn't an accident and won't take the extra money."

"Is it a lot of money?" she asked.

"The difference between six digits and seven digits," Digger said.

"Well, obviously she's crazy," Dolly said with disgust as she swallowed a large portion of her drink.

"Oh, you've met Louise Gillette," Digger said. He put his hand on Dolly's shoulder.

"Gillette, Gillette…I don't think so," Dolly said. "Who died?"

"Her husband in some kind of accident."

"You say," Dolly said.

Digger removed his hand. "Right. He died in some hunting cabin the Belton people own—electrocuted or something."

"Wait. Was that last fall?"

"Yes," Digger said.

"I remember reading about it," Dolly said. "And then there was a lot of talk."

"What kind of talk?"

"People around town. They were saying that what's-his-name, Gillette, he was going to be the next president of Belton and Sons, that's why I remember it."

"You never met Gillette though," Digger said.

She shook her head. "I don't think so."

Digger patted her free hand on the bar. "Too bad," he said. "From what I've heard so far, he was Jack Armstrong and Superman rolled up into one."

She shrugged. Digger squeezed her wrist gently, then released it.

"Is that what you do?" Dolly asked. "Go around, convincing people to take money? I shouldn't think that would be a very hard job under most circumstances."

"No, it wouldn't, but that's not what I do. Actually, I'm an investigator but because they think I'm a little crazy, they give me all the crazies to deal with."

"That man you sent the drink out to today? Was he another one of the crazies?"

"A friend of the family." Digger nodded. "Another crazy. Who owns you?"

"I beg your pardon," Dolly said.

"Today, you said that Eddie, your boss, didn't own you but a lot of people did. Who are the lot of people?" He put his hand on her back, just below the neck.

"You have a good memory, don't you?"

"Yes. And the truth. We're doing truth tonight," Digger said.

"Okay," she said. She paused and took a deep breath as if to enable herself to tell it all at once. "Three years ago, I was doing the housewife number down in Bavington. That's a little town near Pittsburgh. My husband was a plumber. Two kids. House. All very middle America."

"Sounds nice," Digger said. His right index finger touched her fine silky hair.

She nodded. "Yes, it was. My husband was a wonderful man. Kind and thoughtful and…well, he'd do anything for our two kids and me." She paused and looked at her glass before drinking off some of the amber liquid. "Except stop riding his motorcycle. Three years ago, he went over the line and wound up under a truck."

"I'm sorry," Digger said. He opened his hand fully and placed it on the middle of her back.

"You're sorry because you think he died," she said in a flat voice. "I'd be happy if he died. But he didn't. He lived. In a way. Dig, my husband's a vegetable. He can't move. He can't talk. All he can do is sit or lie down. Nothing else. He has to be fed like a baby. He has to be cleaned like a baby."

There was nothing Digger could say so he looked across the room.

"He had no insurance and no pension money. I tried to work, but we lost the house because we couldn't keep up payments. The medical bills were killing me. I had to sell everything. Even my wedding ring. I had to come back here to live with my mother, with him and my two sons. That's who owns me, Digger. My husband, my two boys, my mother, my obligations. Any more questions?"

"I'm sorry, little girl," Digger said. He squeezed her shoulder warmly. "But why the wig? Why the floozy impersonation?"

"When I got here I looked for work. There weren't many jobs then, and those that there were didn't pay enough to eat. I thought about waitressing 'cause I used to do that once, but even those jobs were hard to come by. I even tried up here at this place. An older fellow owned it then. No luck. Then one day, just on an impulse, I bought that wig and did the chorus girl-makeup number and the swishy walk and the push-up bra and I went around applying for jobs. I had to sort out the offers. Eddie's was the best. He gets a lot of driving-through truckers and they tip big for a big-titted smile. And the regulars like to ogle me and make dirty jokes behind my back, and I play stupid and make believe I don't understand. The tips are worth it, so I put up with it. A lot of them don't even know what I really look like or where I live. And I'm careful not to get involved. Telling lies about me is one thing; telling the truth about me would be something else."

"All right. Enough," Digger said. "I'm sorry I brought it up. Let's change the subject. Tell me about Belton."

"Not much to tell. It's a company store. Lucius Belton owns the factories and the plants and the movie theaters and the groceries and the banks, and if you tried to breathe while you're outside, even the air."

"What kind of man is he?" Digger asked.

"I don't know. We don't exactly travel in the same social circles. I saw him once riding in the back of a limousine in a parade. He's as old as death. But I guess he's got something going for him 'cause he's got a young wife and they have a new baby. Can you imagine that? He gave the company a day off when the baby was born. It was like the whole town was closed down. People wandered around the streets and didn't know what to do."

"As long as they didn't try breathing," Digger said. "Did you ever hear anything else about Vernon Gillette?"

"Who?"

"The guy who died in the cabin. The accident," Digger said.

"Hey, you're an investigator. You're not investigating this like it's a murder or something, are you?"

"No, I don't do that kind of work," Digger said. "You never heard anything else about Gillette?"

"No."

They drank together for another hour when Dolly looked at her wristwatch and said, "That's enough drinking. It's getting late."

"You have to go?" Digger asked.

"No," she said.

In his room, Dolly sat almost nervously on the sofa and when Digger sat next to her, she said, "I don't want you to get the wrong idea why I'm here."

"I won't," he said.

"I came here to make love to you," she said.

"Nothing wrong with that idea."

Dolly shook her head. "I wasn't fooling. My husband is paralyzed. He's not a man anymore, but I'm still a woman. Does that make me awful?"

"No," Digger answered, as he was expected to. "That just makes you a woman. A beautiful woman." He touched his hand to her smooth cheek even as he glanced up at the red crystal droplet hanging incongruously from the chandelier. Watch this, Herbie Handlebar, he thought. I bet you weren't this smooth when you climbed into Koko's pants.

"It's just that...well, I know you're just passing through and... well, I can't go having my name..."

He put his index finger across her lips.

"Shhh," he said. "I know. No obligations. No recriminations. Just a need being filled."

She nodded and Digger covered her lips with his as he put his hands under her sweater and around her bare cool waist.

Later she slept, her smooth body plastered to his in sleep as if she feared slipping away from him for even a moment. Digger sipped from his glass of vodka on the end table, then, trying not to move and disturb her, fumbled for his watch. Instead he got hers and in the dim light from the small lamp across the room saw that it was 2:00 A.M. Then, he turned over the gold watch and read the inscription on the back:

To Dolly. Love, Lem.

He wondered if that was her husband's name.

Chapter Six

One of the nice things about being outside of New York was that the farther one got away from the city, the better sausage seemed to taste. Digger thought about this as he ate a breakfast of sausage and eggs in the LaGrande Inn, but could think of no reason for it to be true. So he put it on his list of life's imponderable mysteries along with the purpose of the little red electrical switch on the wall inside everybody's cellar door and why someone would open an eatery and decide, presumably with a straight face, to call it The Terminal Cafe.

Fifteen minutes later, he was driving down into the bowl toward the main headquarters of the Great Belton Dirt Factory.

His tires made a crackling sound as he drove over the grit that coated the driveway and parking lot and everything unfortunate enough to have been stationary in the area for more than twenty minutes.

Lucius Belton and Sons was a compound of buildings, and when Digger got out of his car, he noticed that all the buildings looked alike. He chose the building outside which were parked the largest, newest cars and went in there. He was right. It was the executive office building and he found the personnel department just inside the front door.

There was a young woman sitting at a desk just inside the door. She had enough teeth to make a piano jealous, and Digger wondered if exercise could make teeth bigger because she exercised hers with gum that she snapped as she spoke.

The nameplate on her desk said MISS BUFFET. She was eating with a plastic spoon from a container of yogurt.

"Yeah?" she said to Digger.

"All out of curds and whey?" he said.

"Huh?"

"Never mind. Do you have a guy working here named Vernon Gillette?"

"Sorry, you're out of luck. He died."

"Ohhhh. And I came all this way from Katmandu just to see him. Do you mind if I sit down for a moment? This is an awful shock."

"That far, huh? Well, I'm sorry, but he's dead."

"How'd he die? Did the liquor finally get him? Some husband, I bet. Some woman's husband finally caught up with him and plugged him," Digger said.

"We talking about the same guy?" she said. Snap, snap went the gum. "Vernon Gillette? Nah, he had an accident. Got electrocuted."

"I told him and I told him not to try to change light bulbs by himself," Digger said. "No one ever listens to somebody who's trying to give them good advice."

"You're right, you know," Miss Teeth said.

Digger nodded. "I could tell right off," he said, "that you're the kind of person who'd understand that. Who just wants to help."

She shrugged. Snap, snap. "You have to try, right?"

"Maybe you can help me," Digger said, and instantly the woman's face grew suspicious.

"I'd like to talk to his boss," Digger said.

"Why?"

"I want to know if he said anything about me in his final days. Something I can treasure on my way back to Katmandu. Vernon was my brother, you know."

"Oh. Oh. I didn't know that. I'm really sorry. His boss would be Mr. Spears. He's the head of the planning department. He's in the next building over." She jerked her thumb over her left shoulder. "Just walk over."

Digger stood. "I'll never forget you, Miss Muffet."

"Buffet," she said.

"And then wax it," Digger said as he left.

* * *

"Mr. Spears, please. I was sent over by little Miss Buffet in personnel."

"Your name, please?" The secretary was middle-aged and businesslike. Maybe that was one of the good things, Digger thought, about a business having a seventy-year-old owner. Secretaries were hired because they could secrett, not because they could adorn chairs. And couches.

"Julian Burroughs," Digger said.

"Have a seat, please. You'll have to wait."

The office was small and Digger saw there was no ashtray on the secretary's desk, so he lit a cigarette and blew smoke in her direction, going by what he regarded as the admirable theory that everyone tried to get rid of an obnoxious pest quickly.

After thirty seconds she coughed and after sixty she said, "You can go right in."

Ben Spears was a burly man with a football player's thick neck, displayed in a tieless open-collared shirt. His suit jacket hung on a clothes rack in the corner of the big office. The man's shirt sleeves were rolled up and his thick forearms were matted with dark hair. His desk was cluttered with books, folders and rolled-up sets of blueprints.

He looked up as Digger entered, then, without much interest, said, "Name?"

"Julian Burroughs. I'm with Brokers Surety Life Insurance."

"I don't want any insurance," Spears said, annoyance in his tone. "I thought personnel sent you over. I'm expecting someone from personnel. Are you a planner?"

"More of a conniver actually," Digger said.

"You're not here to discuss a job?"

"No," Digger said. "But if you're looking for work, I can put a word in with my boss. We're a big company. Better yet, call him directly. Walter Brackler. You want his number?"

"I don't want a job," Spears said. "I've got a job. I'm looking for help."

"So few people are willing to help nowadays," Digger said.

Spears's face wrinkled up with puzzlement. "Are you crazy?" he finally said. "You sound like you're crazy."

"No, I'm not crazy," Digger said. "My company had a life insurance policy on Vernon Gillette. I'm just doing some routine checking before we pay up." He noticed that when he mentioned Gillette's name, Spears sat up straighter in his chair.

"All right," Spears said. "Check away. But I don't know what I can tell you."

"Let's find out," Digger said. "You were Gillette's boss?"

"Technically. I'm the head of the planning department. We decide what the company's going to manufacture, whether we're going to build new plants, et cetera. Gillette was in charge of long-range electronic project planning. Technically he was under me, but he reported directly to The Old Man."

"The Old Man being Mr. Belton?"

"That's right," Spears said.

"Was Gillette a good worker?"

"I guess so. Mr. Belton seemed pleased anyway, and that's who you've got to please if you're going to work here."

"I heard that Gillette might have been being groomed to head the company."

"You hear a lot of things," Spears said. "That doesn't make them true." He hesitated a moment, then leaned forward. "Look. It doesn't have anything to do with insurance, I suppose, but I didn't like Gillette. He was The Old Man's fair-haired boy. Maybe he was going to be president. No skin off my nose. I just don't like people working for me that I've got no control over. When he died, well, too bad. It wasn't a tragedy to me. What's this got to do with paying off on his insurance?"

"We had a couple of reports—anonymous reports—at the office that said Gillette didn't die in an accident. He was murdered. I'm checking them out."

"That's his whacky wife," Spears said.

"Mrs. Gillette?"

"What else would his wife be called? Of course, Mrs. Gillette. She's kind of an oddball. I went to the funeral—I had to go—and she was chewing my ear off that Gillette was too smart to die in an accident."

"Was he?"

"Anybody can have an accident," Spears said.

"I've met Mrs. Gillette," Digger said. "I don't think she's too stable."

"Stable? That woman's a walking twitch," Spears said. "Are we almost done? I've got to go get some coffee and I won't be able to keep it down if I have Gillette on my mind. Who the hell would murder him anyway?"

"Maybe somebody who was jealous of him," Digger said blandly. "Maybe some woman's husband. There are always a lot of possibilities."

"By jealous, you mean me?"

Digger shook his head. "I don't mean anybody, Mr. Spears. I'm just kind of looking around to see what I can see. What kind of cabin was that he died in? I understand it's something the company owns?"

"That's right. It's in the hills a few miles outside town. Gillette used it a lot. Company fringe benefit."

"You ever use it?"

"No, I'm not married. I don't have to go out into the woods to cat around."

"Gillette catted around," Digger said as a statement. "I thought so. People I was talking to..."

"I don't know that for a fact," Spears said. "But women were always googah over him. He was good-looking, I'll say that for him. Listen, you sell insurance?"

"My company does."

"I was thinking of buying some. Give me a sales pitch."

"Everybody should be insured," Digger said. "It is the best way for those of us of average means to make sure that our loved ones will be protected if, for any reason, we depart this world before our time. Wouldn't you like to know that your children will be able to go to college and—"

"I don't have kids," Spears said.

"And that your wife won't lose the house you worked so hard to make into a home."

"I told you I'm not married. I live in an apartment."

"Your aging relatives," Digger said. "How will they survive without you?"

"All my family's dead."

"You don't need insurance," Digger said. "Forget it. It's throwing money down a hole. Your company insurance ought to be enough to plant you."

"What company insurance?"

"I thought the company had insurance on its top people," Digger said.

"Not on me. Did they pay for Gillette's insurance?"

"Yes," Digger said.

"See? He was up The Old Man's ass. I don't know, I don't bother with personnel. Maybe they buy insurance for executives with families."

"Maybe," said Digger.

He stood up and said, "I want to thank you for your time. Do you think I could get to see Lucius Belton?"

"He's not in today."

"Tomorrow?"

"I doubt it," Spears said.

"Why?"

"He doesn't like to see anybody," Spears said.

"Why's that?"

"He says everybody's a waste of time. He only likes to see his employees. He says they're too afraid of him to waste his time."

"Are they?"

"You'd better believe it."

Digger had to wait twenty minutes to see Dr. Vincent Leonardo. He read a pamphlet on a table announcing the first annual Well-Baby Examination Program, sponsored by Mr. and Mrs. Lucius Belton, to be held on Sunday, two days away. Digger was finally ushered in after a man wearing a suit and sneakers limped out of the doctor's office.

"Sorry to keep you waiting, Burroughs. I had a particularly virulent case of athlete's foot to deal with."

"If he lives long enough, it'll stop itching," Digger said.

"Oh?"

"Mine did."

Dr. Leonardo, who was listed on the Gillette insurance application as the family physician, was a short, round man in his sixties with a full head of snow-white hair. Incongruously, he wore amber-tinted aviator-style eyeglasses, which gave him the look of the leader of a religious cult that believed marijuana was God in plant form.

"Your nurse told you. I'm here about Vernon Gillette."

"Ah, yes. I imagine you're trying to find some medical cause for Vernon's death so that you won't have to pay Louise for double indemnity."

"Quite an assumption, Doctor."

"I've dealt with insurance companies many times. They are, what we call, slow pay."

"Truth is, Doctor, we want to pay. Mrs. Gillette won't take the money."

"What?"

"It's true. We want to pay the million because it was an accident. She only wants a half a million because it wasn't an accident."

"If it wasn't an accident, what the hell was it?" Dr. Leonardo asked.

"She says maybe a heart attack."

"That's ridiculous. Really, that woman—"

"Let's face it, Doctor. There have been cases of men who looked healthy just suddenly dropping dead of a heart attack, haven't there?"

"Of course there have, Burroughs. And when the autopsy is done, you find out that they had some kind of congenital valve problem that required a plumber or that their arteries were clogged with Elmer's. Glue or something else. Something has to be wrong for somebody to have a heart attack. There was nothing wrong with Vernon's heart."

"Did you do the autopsy, Doctor?"

"Yes. There wasn't a damn thing wrong with him except he wasn't shockproof."

"How well did you know the Gillettes?" Digger asked.

"Well enough. I got them when they first moved up here about two years ago. Lucius asked me to examine Gillette."

"Lucius Belton?"

"Son, in this town there's only one Lucius. Lucius Belton."

"Why did he want you to examine Gillette?"

"I don't think I can tell you that," Leonardo said.

"Let me try to tell you," Digger said. "Just nod if I'm warm. Lucius Belton was grooming Gillette to be the new head of the company. He didn't want him dying on him right after they'd gone to a lot of time and trouble to train him."

"That's accurate," Leonardo said. "You didn't hear it here."

"And when you examined him, he was okay?" Digger asked.

"Better than okay. I sent him down to the University of Pittsburgh Medical Center for three days of tests. They probed and pushed at him." He started ticking off on his fingers. "Heart, lungs, blood, genes, sperm, allergies, mucous secretions, muscle tone, IQ tests, neurology, you name it, they checked it and double-checked it."

"That's pretty much for a physical for a new employee, isn't it?" Digger asked.

"Lucius ordered it. Probably he didn't want to buy any damaged goods."

"Did you examine Gillette after that?"

"Annual physical. I do the whole family. Him and his wife and the daughter."

"And he was okay?" Digger asked.

"Okay. He was perfect. A perfect specimen. No, wait, he wasn't perfect. He had a scar on the back of his right hand. That was it. I tell you, Burroughs, he was Superman."

"Do you think Mrs. Gillette is disturbed?" Digger asked.

"Are we off the record?" Leonardo asked.

"Of course," Digger said. On his right side, he could feel the comfortable vibration of his secret tape recorder whirring.

"No, I don't think so," Leonardo said. "She's one of the most-brilliant people I've ever met. She's just stubborn. The daughter is something else too."

"I know. I've met her. You don't think Vernon Gillette died of—"

"I know—not think, damn it—that he died in an accident. Pay the woman her money, Mr. Burroughs."

Digger stood up. "We're trying, Doctor. Really, we're trying."

Chapter Seven

Someone was watching Digger, and as he got into his car, he saw who it was. A cop in a green-and-yellow prowl car was parked across the street from Dr. Leonardo's.

As Digger pulled his rented Ford away from the curb, he realized he wanted to be home. He didn't want to be in New York talking to Walter Brackler, and he didn't want to be in Pennsylvania driving rented Fords and being watched by policemen and wondering what the hell Koko was doing. He wanted to be back in Las Vegas, driving his own white Mazda, living in his own condominium, drinking in his own favorite saloons, gambling in his own favorite casinos and listening to his favorite records on his own stereo.

Shit on Belton, PA.

In his rearview mirror, Digger saw the patrol car pull away from the curb, make a U-turn and take up a position behind him without pretense. The cop obviously didn't care whether or not Digger knew he was being followed.

The prowl car stayed behind Digger as he drove out of the bowl of Belton. After about five blocks, Digger saw a tavern on the right-hand side of the road. He pulled up to a parking meter, hopped out and walked inside the bar. The police car passed him slowly. Digger stopped to look at it, but the policeman did not meet his eyes.

"Vodka, friend, on the rocks."

"Coming right up."

The surgical tape on Digger's side began to itch, and he went into the men's room to remove the tape recorder.

Digger was alone in the tavern with the bartender—a tall, thin man with unhealthy-looking liver spots on his withered face. His thinning brown hair was kept greased, slicked down and parted absolutely in the middle. Digger thought he looked like a geriatric version of Alfalfa in *The Little Rascals*.

"Just passing through?"

"Yeah," Digger said.

"We don't get many strangers here," the bartender said.

Digger thought, who would you get? The casting director of *That's Incredible?* But he just said, "Guess not." Why was a cop following him? Looking past the bartender into the large mirror behind the bar, he saw the police car pull into a parking spot across the street. Digger wondered if he should send the cop a drink the way he had with Cody Lord. He decided not to. He usually preferred to work with cops instead of antagonizing them.

The bartender was talking. It was either weather or sports, Digger knew. He tuned in a couple of words and heard "air inversion," and he knew it was weather and he really didn't care.

"Mmmm, I guess," he mumbled, without conviction or inflection, knowing there was no statement or question in the world that could not be answered by those three sounds. Then he asked the bartender for change of a dollar and directions to the telephone.

He called the operator and gave her Koko's number in Emporium and charged the call to his credit card. There was no answer.

The operator said, "There's no answer."

"I can hear there's no answer," Digger said. "Let it ring a little more. They may be having a tea ceremony in the backyard."

But it rang a long time without answer and Digger hung up the phone angrily. Maybe he should look up Sluggo Slaphammer's telephone number and call him. He'd probably know where Koko was.

He ordered another vodka and put ten dollars on the bar. The bartender refilled his glass and gave him eight dollars change. Well, they might not have Finlandia vodka in Belton, PA, but at least they had the prices right, Digger thought.

The bartender stood in front of Digger, as if waiting for him to say something. The silence finally got so oppressive that Digger said, "Nice town. But don't you mind the smoke?"

"What smoke?"

"That white stuff in the air," Digger said.

"Oh, *that* smoke. After a while you don't even notice it no more."

"Lucius Belton's smoke," Digger said.

"What does he care? He doesn't smell it," the bartender said. He leaned forward as if to say something confidential. "It's the prevailing westerlies," he said.

"What is?"

"Old Lucius, he ain't no fool, he ain't. He's got a house way up on the west end of the town. High up on the hill. The wind blow from behind his house and it blows that goldern smoke all over everybody else, but none of it don't ever reach him. Old Lucius, he ain't so stupid."

The cop was still there in the mirror.

"How would I find his house?" Digger asked.

"Iffen you went out my door here and turned right and kept going up this road straight, never no mind how much it twisties and turns, and then later the road stops at a crossroad. And right acrosst that crossroad there's a big pair of gates and that's old Lucius's house. Right there. Heh, heh. He lives behind gates. He allus did, but it didn't do him any good when we was kids 'cause I still used to whup his butt. I never liked him much then. I still don't. But don't tell him that. He owns this building."

When Digger drove away, the policeman made another U-turn and followed him. He stayed a half block behind him as Digger drove up the snaking road toward the top of the bowl. After about five minutes, the road ended in a T with a crossroad. On the other side, Digger saw high iron gates. Digger crossed the road, made a sharp left turn and parked on the side of the road, near the gates.

Suddenly the police car's lights and siren came on and it whipped up and pulled in ahead of him.

Digger stayed behind the wheel. On an impulse, he reached into his jacket pocket, took out his tape recorder, turned it on and put it on the floor under the front seat.

The policeman was walking back toward Digger's car. He was not tall, but he was gallows wide and square across the shoulders. His light brown uniform shirt was rolled up to massive biceps. He was wearing a trooper-style hat, and Digger wondered why he wasn't wearing mirror-style sunglasses.

Digger rolled down the car window as the cop approached.

"Driver's license, Mac," the cop said, extending a meaty hand.

Digger fished in his wallet for his license.

"What's the trouble, Officer?" Digger said. He handed the license to the cop, who was red-faced and looked to be about forty, with a broad flat nose and a watery look to his pale blue eyes. His jaw seemed wider than his temples.

The policeman said nothing, but examined the license so long that Digger thought he was trying to memorize it. His shoulder patch read Belton P.D., Digger noticed.

"From Las Vegas, huh?" the cop said.

"Yes."

"You're a long way from home."

"I think I took a wrong turn at Akron," Digger said.

No sense of humor. The cop's mouth was twisted in a surly snarl. "You got anything that states what your business is in town here?"

"You've been following me for an hour. You probably know who I am and why I'm in town."

"Maybe, but I'd like to see something with writing on it."

"Go find a bathroom wall," Digger said. "This is America. You don't need a pass to travel around."

"I love a wise guy, Burroughs. Now you get out of the car and spread 'em."

"You've got to be kidding, Wyatt Earp."

The policeman pulled a heavy revolver from his holster. It looked like a cannon to Digger. He held it nonchalantly in his right hand and said, "Burroughs. Out."

"You're waving a gun at me," Digger said, more for the tape recorder than for the policeman's benefit.

"That's right. Now do you think I'm kidding?"

"I don't think you're kidding," Digger said as he opened the car door. "I just think you're stupid."

The cop's eyes went cold, and Digger realized that the husky man could pull the trigger and no one would see him and then he could make up any kind of story he wanted.

"Put your hands on top of the car right now before I do something you'll be sorry for."

Digger noticed that the policeman did a sloppy job of frisking him.

"Private eye without a piece?" the cop growled. "What's the matter, shamus, you afraid of guns?"

"Only in the hands of an idiot," Digger said. "And nobody says shamus anymore. That went out with Sam Spade."

The cop's face turned red. He snarled, "Keep it up and you might go out any minute yourself." For a moment Digger thought the man was going to swing at him with the gun. But the cop restrained himself.

"We'll leave your car here, Burroughs. I'll take you into town."

"Thanks anyway, but I'm not ready to go back to town yet."

"Yes, you are." The policeman gestured with the gun. "In my car. Now."

"You mind telling me where we're going?"

"Sure. Mr. Belton is a very special man around here, and we don't take kindly to prowlers trying to bother him."

"Prowlers. Because I'm driving on a public road in broad daylight, I'm a prowler?"

"That's right. And you're coming with me."

Digger insisted on locking up his car. His tape machine should have picked up the whole conversation, and when it reached the end of the tape, it would turn itself off. He grabbed his jacket off the seat, locked the car door and walked ahead of the policeman to the squad car.

The policeman's name was Deputy L. E. Harker.

"Deputy what?" Digger asked.

"Just Deputy."

"It figures," Digger said.

They were in a small interrogation room in the basement of an old ramshackle two-story building that housed Belton's finest. Digger was seated in a chair while Harker leaned with his back against the door.

"You been around here a couple of days asking a lot of questions," Harker said. "What are you up to, Burroughs?"

"All right, Harker, let's get something straight. You're not dealing with one of your half-witted townies that you can bluster around with and flex your muscles at so you can get your rocks off. In ten minutes, give or take five, I can have five hundred lawyers down here and I'll be out and your ass will be in front of a grand jury explaining why you committed a false arrest. So let's just stop the bullshit and you tell me what you want, so I can get the fuck out of here because your ugly face is making me sick."

Harker's face had been red before, but now it became crimson. He walked toward Digger, who stood up as the husky, ugly cop got closer. Digger was a half foot taller than the policeman, but not nearly so wide. The policeman's hand was slipping around behind him where Digger knew he carried a blackjack.

"Pull that thing out and I'll shove it up your ass," Digger said.

Harker stopped and growled, "You take a lot of chances."

"I don't think so. I think you're under orders to harass me and find out what I'm doing here, but I don't think anybody told you to go farther than that, so I don't think you'll do a goddamn thing except blather."

"You think that?"

"I'm walking out of here, Harker."

"You're under arrest, Burroughs. You ain't walking nowhere."

"Harker, I think you ought to make a phone call to whoever is doing your thinking for you. Tell him I get one phone call, and that'll go to Frank Stevens, the president of BSLI. He'll be here with lawyers, the FBI and the state police inside of fifteen minutes."

There was confusion on Harker's face. His hand still hovered near the blackjack.

"Make the call, Harker. Make a decision on your own and you're going to screw it up."

Their eyes locked for a few seconds. Digger could see the doubt in his face. Finally, Harker said, "Sit down, Burroughs, and wait."

He stomped out of the room and Digger walked over to a bulletin board where there was a clipboard with pictures of wanted criminals. He glanced through them, thinking that police photography made everybody look-like a criminal. It was the straight-on lighting that flattened out everyone's features and made them look like grave robbers.

The door opened again and Harker came back inside.

"What are you doing over there?" he snapped.

"Looking for your picture. I thought there might be a reward on you."

"I don't like you, Burroughs."

"You hide it well," Digger said.

"You better get your ass out of here before I change my mind," Harker said.

"If you get a chance to change it, do it," Digger said. "Any change'll be an improvement." He picked up his wallet and keys from the desk.

"You going to be on my tail again?" Digger asked. "What are your orders now?"

"Move it, Burroughs."

Digger strolled casually toward the door.

"One more thing," Harker said.

"What's that?"

"Mr. Belton will see you tomorrow at the plant. At noon."

"So that's who you called," Digger said.

"At the plant. At noon."

"You can call Mr. Belton back," Digger said. "I don't remember appointing you my social secretary. You tell him if he wants to meet me, he can call me for an appointment. I'm at Gus's LaGrande Inn. If he can't reach me, leave a message. I'll call him back if I get time."

"This is Julian Burroughs. Let me speak to Brackler."

"Just a moment, I'll see if he's in."

"Why do we always have this conversation?" Digger said. "Of course he's in. Put him on the telephone."

"Just a moment, I'll see if he's in," the secretary repeated stubbornly.

"You've got ten seconds. Then I'm hanging up. Ten, nine, eight, seven, six..."

Brackler came on the line.

"Burroughs, where the hell are you?" he said.

"Where do you think? In Belton, PA."

"Don't you ever call in?"

"I thought that's what I was doing right now," Digger said.

"You talk to that dip? What did she say?"

"She said she wouldn't take the million, but she'd sign a waiver relieving us of all liability in the matter."

"Well, hell, that's not *too* bad," Brackler said.

"If you liked that, you'll love this," Digger said. "I don't think Gillette died in an accident."

"Oh? You're going to tell me heart attack too? That woman's nuttiness is catching?" Brackler said.

"No," Digger said. "But I think maybe he was murdered."

Brackler let out a long, slow sigh. "Oh, Burroughs," he said, "why must you complicate everything? Get out of that town. Let her sign her damned waiver and forget everything."

"I can't," Digger said.

"Why not?"

"I have to protect the company's money. That's the difference between us loyal company types and you guys who are just in it for the bucks."

"Digger, the amount's the same. If he was murdered, we pay five hundred thousand. If she signs a waiver, we pay five hundred thousand."

"Not necessarily," Digger said. "Suppose she killed him? Maybe we get off the hook for nothing?"

"Mmmm," Brackler mmmmmed. "Well, maybe it'd be worth your staying an extra day or two. But let me know what's happening."

"Of course. Don't I always?"

"No, you don't," Brackler said. "By the way, did you give out my home phone number?"

"To whom?" Digger asked.

"Some fagola waiter. Or I think he was a waiter. He kept inviting me out to eat."

"Don't do it, Kwash. No matter how attracted you are to him, don't do it. Nothing good can come of this union."

Chapter Eight

DIGGER'S LOG:

And now it has come to this. Against my better judgment, nay, against my will, I am going to have to stay in Belton, PA, to find out exactly what the Christ is going on here. I hate this. World, do you hear me? I hate this. I come out here to have a nice little vacation with my girl friend. Right? Yes, right. And what happens? She's busy getting her brains screwed out by Sloppo Hugmeyer. She doesn't want to see me. All right. I can deal with that.

What I cannot deal with is some gibboney of a would-be policeman trying to rough me up. I cannot deal with Lucius Belton getting cute with me. I came here to talk to somebody to try to get her to take some insurance money, for Christ's sake, and here I am, almost arrested, harassed, having people keep whispering in my ear, murder, murder, and now I've got to follow that wherever it takes me.

I bet Kwash knew there was something fishy about this. I don't trust him. Kwash, when I die, I'm going to leave you all my tapes so you can feel guilty about how miserable you made me in this life. Play this one over and over again, Kwash. I hate you, Walter Brackler. I've hated you since the first day you were smuggled into the country under Primo Carnera's foreskin. I will always hate you. From the grave, Kwash, imprecations and abominations and curses upon you and your family, yea, even unto seven generations.

That'll fix your ass.

I'm coming back to this. I have to get a drink first.

* * *

Okay, that's better.

Two more tapes in the master file—and I had the insane naïveté to believe there wouldn't even be a master file. Hah!

Tape Number One is Ben Spears, director of planning for Lucius Belton and Sons. He was Vernon Gillette's nominal boss. But Gillette answered only to The Old Man. In capital letters. I bet they don't call Belton that to his face. He's seventy or something. You always call the commander The Old Man in capital letters when he's a young man. When he really gets to be an old man, in small letters, then you call him The Chief or something like that. Maybe I will meet with him and call him The Old Man to his face. In both small and capital letters.

Anyway, Ben Spears didn't like Vernon Gillette. He was jealous of him and his access to the boss. And Ben Spears doesn't have any company insurance. Why did Gillette have it? Spears anyway confirmed what I thought. The Belton hunting cabin in the hills was a little love nest away from home. If Gillette was really murdered, count on it. It was by some broad that he conned into coming up there, and then she couldn't get off.

"Excuse me, miss, do you have any books on female orgasms? Yes, sir. Come with me."

So I got Ben Spears on tape and I have Dr. Vincent Leonardo, who confirmed that Gillette was perfect in every way. Oooops, no. He had a scar on his right hand. He probably got it from trying to rub off the Good Housekeeping Seal of Approval. And Dr. Leonardo thinks that Louise Gillette is a bit of a screwball too. Everybody does. So did Ben Spears.

Leonardo did the autopsy. No heart trouble. No trouble of any kind judging from the physical they gave Gillette before he came to work at Belton and Sons.

Okay, that's Tape One.

I apologize for the quality of Tape Two. It was made through the window of a car while Deputy Dawg was trying to browbeat me. I hate that ugly cop. I hated him on sight. First time ever. Not even you, Kwash, qualified for that honor, but this guy made it. I lust for the moment when I square things with him.

Deputy Dawg Harker, it seems, was sicced on me by Lucius

Belton—first to follow me and then to stop me if I got close to Belton's house. Why?

I don't know why.

And how did Belton even know I was in town? Everybody talks around this damned town. I doubt if there's a person left who doesn't know who I am and what I want.

Maybe I'll meet with Lucius Belton tomorrow and maybe I won't. Let him call me, if he wants to. I may just stay around this town forever, annoying people, living in this room, looking up at that silly red dot on the chandelier and trying to exorcise the spirit of Sappo Muckenmire.

I do not like the work I do for a living. I was happier when I was a degenerate gambler, living in Las Vegas on what passes for my wits. You've always wondered, Kwash, what I had on Frank Stevens that he ever hired me to work for Old Benevolent and Saintly. Since I'm leaving you this tape in my will and now that I'm dead, I can tell you, Kwash.

I can but I won't. Let you guess on forever. Just let me give you a tip out of the depths of our friendship. If you're ever in Las Vegas and you meet the president of an insurance company and he's just been ripped off for five hundred thousand dollars in negotiable securities, don't volunteer to get them back from the hooker who swiped them. I won't say I did that, Kwash, but if I did, look where it got me.

Expenses. Gas, twenty dollars. All that driving up and down Belton's dirt bowl. Drinks to wash away the dirt and to research the intrinsic socioeconomic factors and the infrastructure that makes Belton, PA, such a unique American community, twenty-five dollars. Eight bucks for the cab to take me back to my car after that idiot cop hauled me in. Fifty bucks to try to bribe Deputy Dawg, who took the money, didn't report it and took me in anyway. Total, one hundred and three dollars, and the day has only just begun. And don't think that's the end of it. If I suffer permanent emotional trauma from being threatened today, you guys are going to have to pay for the shrink. Maybe I'll take my ex-wife and What's-his-name and the girl. We can probably get a group rate.

See how upset I am. I forgot to say that this is Tape Recording Number Two, it's 7:00 P.M., Friday, there's still no answer at Koko's house, and I am going to take a shower and wash away this crud and then, maybe, slip off someplace to have a nice cocktail before my drinks.

If you're listening to this, Kwash, it means I'm dead. Think kindly of me. Remember. I always tried to do my best.

Chapter Nine

Downstairs, Gus told Digger that there had been a phone call for him.

"Why didn't you put it through? I was in my room."

"He didn't want to be put through."

"He?"

"Yeah. Some guy. He wouldn't give his name."

"What was the message?" Digger asked.

"Orleans."

"Orleans?"

"That's right. Orleans."

"What the hell is Orleans?" Digger asked.

"There's a jazz club outside town called Orleans. Maybe that's what he meant."

"You better tell me exactly what he said."

Gus said, "He called about fifteen minutes ago. He said he wanted to leave a message for Julian Burroughs. I said I'd ring your room. He said, no, he just wanted to leave the message. I said, okay what's the message? He said Orleans. I said, just like you did, Orleans? And he said it again, Orleans; then he hung up."

"No name?" Digger asked.

"No."

"Did he sound old? I'm expecting a call from Lucius Belton."

"No, I know Belton's voice. It wasn't him. I don't know who it was."

Gus gave him the directions to the Orleans jazz club, and as Digger walked out to the car, he wondered who had called and why.

It wasn't Koko, which was the only call he wanted, and it wasn't Lucius Belton. Who? Cody Lord? Ben Spears? Doc Leonardo? Deputy Dawg? It could have been anybody. It seemed like everyone in town knew he was visiting. Maybe it was Huckleberry Slockbower calling to give the name of the latest maid he had deflowered. And what kind of ridiculous word was "deflower," anyway?

It was probably Cody Lord.

Inside the Orleans, a four-piece combo labored with "Perdido." The music was bad but blessedly low-volumed. A dozen people sat around the big inside room at tables, but the bar was empty. The bartender looked at Digger as if he resented his disrupting the pristine, empty purity of his establishment.

"Vodka, rocks. You have Finlandia?"

"No."

"Anything as long as it's not Russian."

When the bartender brought the drink, Digger said, "Start me a tab. I think I'll be here awhile."

The bartender stuck the bill in the bar molding in front of Digger.

"Maybe you can help me with something," Digger said.

"That's why I'm here."

"A friend of mine, Vernon Gillette—"

"That's easy. He's dead."

"He used to hang out here?" Digger asked.

"Yeah."

"I never knew he liked jazz."

"He liked our piano bar," the bartender said.

"Oh?"

"You'll see why when this set is over," the bartender said.

Digger was two drinks into the evening when the quartet finished, almost simultaneously. The spotlights that had illuminated the musicians' stage went off and another dim light came on in a corner of the room, shining on a small grand piano with a bar built around it. Digger picked up his drink and headed for the piano bar.

He sat at the seat closest to the piano's bass notes. He was alone there, and he felt like a fool, sitting in the spotlight. Maybe he should hop up on the piano's top and tap dance. Fred Astaire always looked good doing it. Somehow he doubted that Fred Astaire ever had to pay later for a new piano top. Kwash wouldn't go for a piano top.

The light came on brighter and Digger felt somebody brush behind him. He turned to see a woman with shoulder-length flame-red hair, wearing a green evening gown cut so low that her bosom seemed ready to spill out.

She could have been thirty or she could have been forty. She had a tiny cherub's face with cupid's bow lips. Tiny laugh wrinkles at the outside corners of her eyes seemed to tell more about her sense of humor than her age. She nodded at Digger as she squeezed by him and sat at the piano.

Digger asked a waitress for a refill "and one of whatever the lady here drinks." The pianist nodded approval to the waitress, then said to Digger, "Never saw you here before."

"Never been here before," Digger said. "A friend of mine told me about this place…and its attractions."

She started to play softly the opening chords of "Everything Happens to Me."

"Who was that?"

"Old school chum. He died. Vern Gillette."

He heard just a moment's delay in her smooth piling-up of chords, then she caught herself and mumbled to Digger, "Later," and put her attention back on the piano.

She played smoothly, toying with the outlines of the melody, pumping into it clusters of tight packed ten-finger chords. In the center of the number, she built the song up to crescendos that would have seemed appropriate for a concert stage, and then she began to peel away, one at a time, each of the blocks in the musical house she had built until she was back to the basic melody, playing it clean and uncluttered and simple, with an elegant power that she could not have captured if she had attacked the piano with both fists flying, like a lumberjack running amok in the forest.

She finished to a light smattering of applause and looked at Digger, almost shyly, as if beseeching him for approval.

"I knew I'd find it if I looked hard enough," he said.

"What's that?"

"Something classy in Belton, PA."

"Thank you, thank you, thank you," she said and cocked her head to the side in a parody of a bashful child. It was a cute gesture and it made her not one bit less lovely. Digger liked women who could do cute.

When the waitress returned with the drinks, the pianist and Digger clicked glasses.

"Cheers," she said.

"To good friends," he said.

"If we're good friends, I ought to know your name."

"Walt," Digger said. "Walt Brackler."

"I'm Marla Manning."

"I know. Vern mentioned you to me," Digger said.

"He did? What'd he say?"

"He told me you were beautiful and talented."

"How nice."

"Vern was always given to understatement," Digger said. "He didn't tell me how beautiful or how talented."

"Careful, Walt, I may steal you from your wife."

"Sorry. The divorce courts beat you to it." He raised his glass again. "Here's to divorce courts."

"Listen to the music," she said. "After this set, we can talk."

"My pleasure," Digger said.

They were at a table in a dark corner.

"Yeah, sure," Digger was saying. "Vern and I were in college together out in California. It's funny, you know, how he always had this image of Mr. Absolutely-Straight-as-a-Dime, but when he wanted to be, he was a wild man."

"I know," Marla said.

"So we surfboarded and partied and clowned our way through California. It was just like him, though. He graduated magna cum laude and I barely sneaked out. Then he came east and I stayed west, but we stayed in touch all these years. You don't like to lose a good friend."

"No, you don't. What do you do, Walt?"

"I got hooked up with a tool company out on the coast. Slaphammer Incorporated. I'm kind of a troubleshooter."

"Oh. What kind of troubleshooter?" she asked.

"If you've got any trouble, I'll shoot it," Digger said. "Heh, heh, only kidding. Tell me, what's a nice dish like you doing in a sink like this?" But he already knew the answer. For the last half-hour, Marla Manning had been matching him drink for drink. He knew very few men who could do that for long, and no women. It was just simply a matter of body size. Digger was almost twice as big as most women. Even if he hadn't had a natural talent with alcohol, it still would have taken twice as much liquor to bring him down as it would have taken for a smaller woman. That Marla Manning was trying to stay with him told him all he needed to know about her problems.

She searched his face across the candlelit table. The quartet was playing softly in the other corner of the room.

"Oh, I've worked around," she said. "Then I kind of lost my energy, scratching out a living in a lot of places. And I knew I wasn't going to be a star."

"You're good," he said honestly.

"But not great. I'm not Evans or Oscar or Tatum or Thelonious. They're genius and I'm good. I used to try. I was young and I was in love and I was doing the dope and the booze. A young guitar player. He was beautiful—Christ, was he beautiful. But he was a junkie. And we played our lives away in this hazy kind of mist. I never knew that he was dying, a little bit every day, right in front of my eyes. One night, he got really sick and I was taking him to the hospital in my car. It's a wonder I didn't drive into a building—I was so zipped. Then there was this awful sound and I looked over and blood was gushing out of his mouth, like a fire hydrant just turned on, and it was all over the car and all over me. He died on me, just like that, in some shitty car, in some ratty-assed section of the East Village, and I said to myself, you're next. So I got straightened out and I came up here about five years ago. I've got steady work and I like what I do. I still drink too much. Maybe if I were great instead of just good, maybe I wouldn't, I don't know. But I do and I can live with it. At least I'm going to die in bed. I'm going to be a hundred years old and I won't have a tooth in my face, but I'll die with a smile and a bottle in my hand. It beats dying blowing your guts up in some rotten car in some rotten city."

Digger covered her hand with his. "I'm sorry," he said. "I didn't mean to bring up something unhappy."

She smiled sadly, then looked out the window as if there was a future there where everybody was a genius and nobody died hemorrhaging in autos. Digger didn't let go of her hand.

"Vern was special to you, wasn't he?" Digger said.

She nodded, still looking away. "I loved him, Walt."

"He loved you too."

She turned back. "Did he ever say that, Walt?"

"He didn't have to. It was all over his letters. Hell, the way he talked, well, tell the truth, I thought you two were going to hook up someday. Marriage, the whole thing."

She shrugged. "Would have been nice. You know, we got together right after he got up here, and it was funny, we really used to have to sneak around 'cause Vern said he was going to be president of the company or something and what's-his-name, Lucius Belton, wouldn't hold still for any hanky-pank. Then it all went sour."

"How sour?" Digger asked.

"After a while, it seemed like Belton didn't have any use for him anymore. That's what Vern said. It was like they were ignoring him, wishing he'd go away."

"Why was that?" Digger asked.

"He didn't know. Didn't he tell you about it?"

"You know Vern," Digger said. "He liked to put a good face on things. I just never got the sense from his letters that anything was wrong. It's funny, though. With the pressure off him from the company, why not marriage?"

"I was afraid to ask," she said. "Afraid he'd think I was pushing too hard. So it was Wednesday and Saturday for a year and a half. They were good Wednesdays and Saturdays, Walt. We never missed one. I'm ready for another drink."

"I've been waiting for you," Digger said.

"A man after my own heart."

"It's not just your heart I'm after," Digger said and Marla squeezed his hand.

By unspoken arrangement, Digger knew he was to wait for her to finish work that night. He watched her from the corner table and thought that she just might be wrong about herself. If she wasn't great, she was awfully close to it.

During her second set, he found the telephone and called Gus's LaGrande Inn.

"Julian Burroughs, Gus. Any calls for me?"

Gus's voice was excited. "Hey, Lucius Belton called. Himself. He left a number for you to call. You know, he didn't give his name, but I could recognize his voice. I didn't know if I should tell him to try the Orleans. Is that where you are?"

"Yeah."

"I didn't know whether to tell him to try there, but he didn't give his name or anything so I didn't."

"You done good, Gus," Digger said. "No call from a woman?"

"No."

Where the hell was Koko?

Digger called the number Lucius Belton had left and when a man's voice said hello, Digger knew how people could recognize Belton's voice over the telephone. The voice was crackly and high-pitched, with almost an electric intensity to it. It was the kind of voice you expected to break out into a cackle any moment.

"This is Julian Burroughs. I was told to call this number."

"I am Lucius Belton."

"Thank you for sending the welcome wagon after me today," Digger said.

"I'm sorry for that. Sometimes people mean well but don't execute well."

"I think Deputy Dawg would have been glad to execute me if you had given the okay. So what do you want?"

"Would you be able to meet with me tomorrow?" Belton asked. Digger had a feeling the man was trying to hold his anger under control.

"What time?"

"Noon at the plant."

"I can't make noon," Digger said perversely. "Eleven-thirty or twelve-thirty would be better. If it's eleven-thirty, I can only give you a half-hour."

"Twelve-thirty then," Belton said. "The security guard will show you to my office."

"All right. Is that all?" Digger asked.

"Yes."

Digger hung up.

Marla Manning did four sets and by the time she finished the last, she was very drunk.

Vernon Gillette had been the second great love of her life. When she'd found out that he had died—she read it in the paper—she went on a solitary binge, drinking in her home for three days.

"When'd you see him last?" Digger had asked.

"I don't remember. Before he died," she said. "If only…"

"If only what?" Digger asked.

She shrugged.

She had not gone to the funeral. She didn't want to see Louise Gillette, couldn't stand the thought of another woman weeping for her Vern.

As they left the Orleans, Marla held tightly to Digger's arm, a grip more frantic than friendly and required by her obvious inability to walk very well.

"My car's over here," Digger said.

"'s all right," she said. "I just live across the street. No car. Unless you going to park in my living room." She giggled.

"Okay. I'll walk you over," Digger said.

"Everybody walks me over," she said. "That's not what I mean. Mean men walk over me. All my life. They walk over me and then they die on me."

"I won't," Digger said. He helped her up the steps of the small house and waited while she fumbled for her key.

"You're coming in for coffee," she said.

"Well, I…"

"Walt, you're coming in for coffee. What are friends for if they don't have coffee? Anyway, you can't drive in that condition. You're too blurry already." She giggled again.

Marla led him into her living room, a heavy leaden room decorated around a grand piano and a lot of plants that seemed to be on the verge of death.

"I gotta go tinkle," she said.

"I'll make the coffee," Digger said. He was glad the bathroom was on the first floor because he wouldn't have trusted her trying to find her way up a flight of steps.

He put a saucepan of water on the stove to boil, and found instant coffee in a cupboard over the built-in wall oven. He used the lid of the coffee jar as a spoon to put some coffee into two clean cups he found on the sink.

When Marla came back into the kitchen, Digger was standing by the stove, counting.

"Fifteen, fourteen, thirteen…"

"What are you doing?"

"I'm giving that water twenty more seconds to boil. If it doesn't, I'm using it anyway."

"That's stupid," she said.

"The hell it is," Digger said. "I always do that. You've just got to make up your mind who's running things. You or water. Twelve, eleven, ten, nine…"

"This way you get cold coffee."

"Sometimes," Digger admitted. "But you don't get high blood pressure from being frustrated by water."

"Get out of my kitchen. I'll make the coffee."

They sat on her couch sipping their coffee. Marla had her head on Digger's shoulder; his arm was draped loosely around her. But instead of sobering her up, the coffee seemed to make her more drunk.

She turned her head and said to Digger, "You're spending the night, aren't you?"

"If you want," he said.

"I want." She reached up and pulled his hand down around her shoulder and into the top of her dress, then pressed it with her own hand against her opulent breast.

Three minutes later she was asleep and Digger extricated himself from her, arranged her on the couch, put a pillow under her head and covered her with a handmade afghan he found draped across the back of a chair.

He sipped her coffee. She had laced it with brandy. In the kitchen, he washed out both cups, then turned out the lights and let himself out of the house.

He had taken advantage of her enough already tonight.

Chapter Ten

DIGGER'S LOG:

Tape Recording Number Three, 3:30, Saturday A and M, Julian Burroughs in the matter of Vernon Gillette and his wife, Casey Jones.

If anybody asks me what college I went to, from now on I'm going to tell them I went to Saturday A and M. I never get a good night's sleep. I think that this is what is really wrong with me. I'm always tired. If that's so, why can't I fall asleep when I try to?

All right, Marla Manning was Vern Gillette's little piece on the side. I like him better already because it's nice, first of all, to know that Superman had a hole in his sock, and, second, that he had some taste. Marla is all right and Vern couldn't be that bad because she fell in love with him and she didn't fall in love with me, and women always fall in love with me. I don't think she fell in love with me.

I've got to thank that simp, Cody Lord, for sending me to Orleans. Of course it was him. Who else knew that I might have some interest in a Vernon Gillette girl friend. How like him to do it anonymously. But if he thought it was going to nail down the murder theory, he's wrong. I don't pick Marla as a murderer. But there were those two unmade beds in the cabin. Was Marla in one of them? I couldn't find out. Not yet, anyway.

I've got to remember now, she thinks my name is Walt Brackler. Why do I do that? It's strange how in moments of psychological stress, I take refuge in my insanity.

Marla is, in fits and starts, on Tapes Three and Four, now added to my permanent library of nice people who have known me.

She said something interesting, that Gillette had started out cozy and warm with Lucius Belton and then their relationship cooled. I've got to ask The Old Man about that today in, God, nine more hours when I meet with him.

Expenses since the last time I lied. Sixty dollars for drinks with Marla Manning. Why do I always meet women who drink?

And why didn't Koko call?

Chapter Eleven

As Digger got out of his car in the almost-empty parking lot of Lucius Belton and Sons, a uniformed guard approached him.

"Mr. Burroughs," he said.

"Yes."

"Would you follow me?"

"Sure. How'd you know it was me?"

"I had your license plate numbers. They checked."

Sure, they had his license plate, Digger thought. And probably his age, weight, school records, dental charts and personal habits. Lucius Belton didn't go places in half steps.

"In the name of Lucius, the Sons and the Belton Works, amen," Digger muttered.

Inside a low building set back from the parking lot, Digger was handed over to a well-dressed young man with "executive assistant" stamped all over him.

"Burroughs?" the man said. His smile was all teeth and his clothes all neat creases.

"Good guess," Digger said.

"You're expected. I'm Johnson, Mr. Belton's assistant."

"Of course you are."

"Please follow me." He led the way down a long hall lined with expensive ugly oil paintings of rich, ugly men. Were these the Beltons?

"These paintings," Digger said.

"Yes, sir?" said Johnson, stopping short.

"It looks like a set for a Vincent Price movie."

Johnson cleared his throat. "You seem to have an active sense of humor," he said.

"I'm actually a stand-up comic," Digger said. "I'm only working for the insurance company on the side until my career takes off."

"I see," said Johnson seriously. "Actually Mr. Belton is not keen on active senses of humor. You might think about keeping yours in check while you are in the presence."

"The presence"? Did he really say that, Digger wondered.

"Of course," Digger said. "Somber will be the order of the day. I can really do somber. Once you learn to fake sincerity, everything else is easy. But you would know that, wouldn't you?"

Johnson led him past a secretary with no redeeming qualities and tapped lightly on a heavy oak door. He opened the door and said, "Mr. Burroughs, sir," then stood aside so Digger could enter. When Digger was inside the room, the door closed silently behind him.

Lucius Belton was sitting behind a desk between two banks of long windows in the far corner of the room. He was absolutely bald, but it was not the bald head of someone who shaved his scalp under the mistaken impression that it made him look better. Belton's baldness had the look of being caused by terminal eczema. His face was fleshless, almost as if skin had been stretched drumhead tight over his skull. His nose was a large, sharp protrusion from between sunken cheeks, and his thin lips were exactly the same pasty color as the rest of his face. His eyes were pale and watery inside deep sockets, and when his lips drew back to speak, Digger could see that he had long, narrow, yellowed teeth with spaces between them. Digger could not remember ever seeing anything or anyone uglier, outside of something kept in a jar on a laboratory shelf.

Belton stood up when Digger approached the desk. He moved stiffly, as if his spinal column were made of glass and he had to be extra careful not to chip it.

Through his shirt, Digger turned on his tape recorder.

"Good to see you, Burroughs," Belton said in that thin, high-pitched snarl of a voice.

"I'm glad you're happy," Digger said. "Does this mean you won't try to have me arrested again?"

"Sit down," Belton said and pointed to a chair. He made no effort to shake hands, and as Digger sat down, he looked around the room. The walls were devoid of all decoration. They were dark, dead oak, much like their inhabitant, Digger thought.

"I already apologized for the zealousness of Deputy Harker," Belton said sharply. "I only apologize once."

"That must make it tough on the world if you fuck up twice," Digger said.

Belton cleared his throat. Just like his executive assistant, Digger thought. Maybe everybody in Belton, PA, cleared their throats a lot. Living on soot might make it an essential survival skill. Not that there was any soot inside this office. Digger felt the chill of built-in air conditioning pumping clean, cold air into the office.

"You have been asking questions about the death of my friend and employee, Vernon Gillette," Belton said.

"That is correct."

"Do you mind if I ask why?"

"Do you mind if I don't answer?" Digger said.

"Why is that?"

"My business is between Mrs. Gillette and my insurance company. I don't see that you have any involvement in it at all," Digger said.

"I paid the premiums on that insurance," Belton said. He seemed suddenly to realize he was still standing behind his desk, holding on to it tightly with blue-tinged fingers, and he sat down slowly. "I think I have a right to make sure that your insurance company is acting properly."

Digger thought about that for a moment and thought also that he wanted Lucius Belton to talk, so he nodded and said, "Perhaps you're right about that."

Belton nodded back, as if to say, yes, of course, he was right; he was always right, and it was the shame of lesser human beings that they didn't always seem to understand that point.

"Is there some difficulty about your company paying off on the policy?"

"Have you spoken to Mrs. Gillette since her husband died?" Digger asked.

"Not directly. I saw her at the funeral, of course, and offered to help her in any way I could. She didn't ask for anything, so I haven't talked to her. Why is that pertinent?"

"Because Mrs. Gillette refuses to take our million dollars. She insists that Gillette died of a heart attack, not in an accident."

"But it was an accident," Belton said. "Surely she must—"

"Do you know the lady?" Digger interrupted.

"Yes."

"Then you know there is nothing 'surely' about anything that touches her."

"I suppose you're right, Mr. Burroughs. It's too bad, though, isn't it? I asked the police to be very thorough. Vern's death *was* an accident. That lady is due one million dollars."

"You know that and my company knows that," Digger said.

"And do you know that?" Digger thought that Belton was sharp. He had caught the slight omission in Digger's voice.

"I did when I arrived here," Digger said. "Now I'm not so sure."

"Why is that, Mr. Burroughs?"

"Some things just don't add up to an accident, Mr. Belton."

"What do they add up to?"

"I don't know yet," Digger said.

"Give me an example of what doesn't add up," Belton said.

"Why did you have a big policy on Gillette's life? You don't have one for your other executives."

"You probably have found out by now that I thought Vern would eventually take over the company. When I hired him, I was the last of the Beltons and, as you can guess, my health is none too good. I negotiated the insurance with him as a fringe benefit. He wanted to be sure that his wife and daughter would be cared for if anything should happen to him."

"And something did happen to him," Digger said. "At the time of his death, was that still your plan? To have him succeed you as president?"

"Yes. Why do you ask?"

"Because I had heard that somehow your relationship with Gillette had cooled off after he came here."

Belton hesitated. "All right. It was Mrs. Gillette, Louise. My wife, Amanda, doesn't like her. Right from the start, she didn't like her. Mrs. Gillette is, well, a strange person. The child, Ardath, is a delight, but Louise...well, you've met her. I guess I don't have to tell you."

"*Whoooo, whooo,*" Digger said, imitating a locomotive.

"Exactly. She is strange and Amanda didn't like her strangeness."

"So what did that have to do with Gillette?" Digger asked.

"It was difficult to be social friends with them because of Louise and my wife. So I sort of stopped inviting the Gillettes over. Probably I shouldn't have done that, Mr. Burroughs, but I love my wife very much. Anyway, I kept very close to Vern around here. He was in my office much of the time."

"Were there any other women in Gillette's life?" Digger asked.

He could see Belton bristle. "No. And I think I would have known."

"Why would you have known?" Digger asked. "People cheat all the time."

"This is a small town," Belton said. "People talk."

"Yes, they do," Digger agreed amiably. "Why did you sic the cops on me?"

"That was a misunderstanding."

"That misunderstanding nearly got me shot. I'd like to know what caused that misunderstanding," Digger said.

"I had heard you were around town."

"From whom?"

"That isn't important," Belton said.

"It is to me," Digger said. "I want to know who to cross off the guest list for my next fox hunt."

"I heard it from more than one person," Belton said. "You don't exactly come quietly in the night."

Digger thought that meant Ben Spears and somebody else. Probably Cody Lord. Or Dr. Leonardo. Somebody who told somebody, who told somebody else.

"Let it pass," Digger said. "Why the cops?"

"I thought you might try to harass me and my family."

"I'm sure it's the first thing on the mind of every insurance investigator who comes to town," Digger said.

"You have to understand, Mr. Burroughs. I am a very wealthy

man. My wife and I are new parents. She worries, perhaps inordinately, that someone will try to kidnap our baby."

Digger nodded.

"So I asked the police to keep an eye on you and not let you annoy my family. That deputy, what is his name?"

"Hog," Digger said.

"Harker. Yes, he stopped you near my house. He shouldn't have done that."

"Why did you want to meet with me today?" Digger said.

"To apologize and explain my actions. To ask you how long you are going to be in Belton."

"I don't know yet."

"You were going to tell me why you thought Vern's death might not be accidental," Belton said.

"It's just an instinct I have in these things," Digger said.

"Your instinct's wrong here," Belton said. "Vern's death was an accident. Heart attack! He was in perfect health. Absolutely perfect."

"Those aren't the only two alternatives," Digger said.

"Oh? What others are there?"

"Suicide," Digger said mildly. "Murder."

Belton looked disgusted and shook his head. Digger half-expected it to fall off.

"That's ridiculous," Belton said. "It was an accident, pure and simple."

"I'll leave when I'm sure of that," Digger said.

"Accident. Accidents can happen to anyone," Belton said. He looked sharply at Digger as if to make sure that the insurance man had understood him.

"You said you had a new son," Digger said. "Then who are the sons in Lucius Belton and Sons?"

"That Lucius Belton was my father. There were four of us sons. I'm the last alive. I was the last Belton until my son, Lucius the third, was born."

"Well, congratulations on your fatherhood," Digger said as he rose from his chair.

"Thank you," Belton said. He rose too. "I wish you could resolve this matter quickly without causing too much disruption."

"I'd like to. I'd like to put it all behind me too," Digger said.

"You'll be staying then," Belton said.

"Until I'm done."

"Well, who knows?" Belton said with a lipless attempt at a smile. "You might be done sooner than you think."

Chapter Twelve

Digger felt chilled coming out of the Belton plant, so he stopped two blocks away for coffee. The diner was empty and the waitress was homely, so Digger bought a newspaper at the cash register so he could make believe he was reading it and not have to talk to her.

He idly turned the pages of the *Belton Bulletin* while he sipped his coffee, but his mind wasn't on the newspaper. He had realized that he was annoying Lucius Belton, but the annoyance seemed now to have grown into a dangerous anger. Why was Belton so upset because Digger was looking into Gillette's death?

And wasn't Lucius Belton something to see? If his name had been Lucifer instead of Lucius, it might have been more apt. The face of a death mask; the body of a dried-out seed pod; the voice a cackle that seemed to come from the dark corners of a darker soul. And he had fathered a child?

Which brought up Mrs. Belton. Someone had told him she was young and that immediately put him on edge. He didn't believe in June-December romances. Scratch a young wife and an old, really old, husband and what you generally found was not love that defied the odds, but monetary arrangements based equally upon female avarice and male stupidity. He put the matter out of his head and concentrated on the *Belton Bulletin*, which he quickly decided was no better and no worse than any other paper he read.

Digger had once been a regular reader of the newspapers, refusing to start a day without the *New York Times* lying on the table, in gray splendor, next to his coffee. But as he got older, he began to understand that newspapers never threw out their old stories; they just reran them later on with different names filling in the blanks.

"Left-wing rebels struck today at a government army installation outside the capital city of (fill in one)."

"The nation's economic indicators moved (up) (down) slightly last month. The announcement from Washington touched off a wave of (buying) (selling) on the New York Stock Exchange."

How had he ever been able to read a newspaper anyway? All that time wasted reading about the world could have been spent changing the world. He saw the waitress hovering over him, ready to snatch his cup as soon as he released it from his fingers.

"Did you know that people who read newspapers never amount to anything?" he told her.

She sneered. "I didn't know it until I saw you reading," she said.

"Very good," he said admiringly. "That's just one class of people who don't count. People who smoke pipes don't amount to anything either."

"My son smokes a pipe."

"Sure he does. And people's names that begin with *P-F.* I never met anybody whose name began with *P-F* who was good for anything. That's because whenever you talk to a person like that, you never listen to him. You're only wondering about how he pronounces his name. Imagine his name is P-F-oopler. Do you call him Mr. Poopler or Mr. Foopler? They don't even know, so how are you supposed to know? The saddest ones of all are the ones who try to pronounce both the *P* and the *F.* They sort of say Puh-foopler. Everybody knows that's ridiculous. How can your name be Puh-foopler?"

"My name is McBride."

"A nice name for a nice lady," Digger said. "If your name were Puh-foopler, you would be on welfare somewhere."

"Welfare? Let me tell you that—"

"Shhhh. Can't you see I'm reading?" Digger said.

There was a small news item in the paper.

MRS. LUCIUS BELTON
TO DEDICATE GALLERY

Mrs. Lucius Belton will officiate at 2:00 P.M. today at the opening of the new Belton Gallery in the town's art museum, located on the remodeled second floor of the town library.

All of Belton's art lovers are invited to attend the ceremony.

Digger glanced at his watch. It was 1:45 P.M.

"Say, where's the town library?" he asked.

"Six blocks down, turn right, four blocks more on the left," the waitress said. She pointed off in a direction.

"Thank you," Digger said. He paid her for the coffee and paper and left a dollar tip, which earned him a glacial smile that indicated she was more thrilled by his departure than by his dollar.

The newspaper had invited all Belton's art lovers to attend the ceremonies, and perhaps all of them had shown up.

Nine.

Plus Digger.

There was one fussy man who looked to Digger like a librarian and eight women, all middle-aged. Three of them looked like employees called out, as at a political rally, to swell the crowd.

They milled around in a central upstairs hallway. At the end of the hallway were a pair of closed double doors, with a pink ribbon strung across them. Apparently, Mrs. Belton was late.

Digger perched on a windowsill near a tall metal ashtray and smoked while he looked out into the street.

Yes, he decided, Lucius Belton was probably hooked by his young wife, but maybe he retained some sense of sanity. If his wife had been able to lead him around by the nose, old man Belton would have made sure the library was packed for the art gallery opening. Marching bands, lines stretching around the corner, people sleeping in front at night to be sure to get an early place in line. In Belton, PA, old Lucius could have done those things if he wanted, Digger knew. But he hadn't. Just a twerpy librarian and eight ladies.

Digger was stubbing out his cigarette when an enormous black limousine turned the corner and rolled up toward the front of the library. It was a black customized Mercedes Benz. Digger had seen one once before on display in a national automobile show.

The vehicle was armored and bulletproof. All the electrical and hydraulic systems were dual, so that if gunfire knocked one out, the other would still work. The radiator was hidden behind steel plates and the fuel tank could withstand direct firearm hits. The car had a built-in fire extinguisher system. Digger remembered hearing the pretty model who was decorating the display say that it was designed to withstand a "NATO Level Five assault," which meant from firearms using armor-piercing ammunition. After the demonstration, Digger had gone up to tell the model that he wanted to buy two of them.

"Two?" she had said.

"Yes. But first, what kind of mileage does it get?"

"Mileage?"

"Yes. How many miles per gallon?"

She looked at a fact sheet in her hand. "Seven," she said.

"Too bad," Digger said. "Cancel the sale. My moped gets a hundred and sixty to the gallon."

"Do you mind if I ask you something?" the model had said.

"Go ahead."

"Are you crazy?"

"Only about you," Digger had said, and invited her to dinner. He still remembered the evening fondly.

The big Mercedes pulled up in front of the library and a uniformed chauffeur hopped out of the driver's seat and ran to the back to open a door. Lucius Belton had said that his wife was afraid of kidnappers; seeing the car now made Digger believe it.

His first view of Amanda Belton was of a long tanned leg stretching out from the back door of the car. It was quite a leg, followed by quite a woman. Amanda was a wondrously slim ash-blonde with a model's face. She wore a pale-tan silk suit, and the afternoon sun hit her hand at just the correct angles to flash diamond sparkles toward Digger. She smoothed her skirt over her hips, said a few words to her driver and walked briskly toward the front door of the library.

Digger guessed her age at thirty-couple, but the thought of her with the withered, devilish wraith that was Belton made her seem even younger. He walked over to join the other nine persons who were clustered around the door to the art room. On the wall, Digger noticed a small plaque that read: "The Belton Gallery, Courtesy of Mr. and Mrs. Lucius Belton. Paintings on loan from The Belton Collection."

He heard the woman's shoes coming up the stairs and saw the little man flit over to her, all butterfly-a-twitter.

"Oooh, Mrs. Belton, how good of you to come. Folks, here's Mrs. Belton."

Amanda Belton nodded to him imperiously and then said some random, casual good-afternoons to the women standing near the door. Her eyes met Digger's and she nodded her head and smiled, very precisely—too much to be called cool; too little to be called forward; just enough of each to be called pleasant.

The little man was running about now, his hands filled with camera and scissors.

Finally he stood by the wall next to the double doors and started waving at people. "Go stand on that side over there. So when Mrs. Belton cuts the ribbon, you'll all be in the background." Digger moved over and stood in the middle of the eight women. He thought it would make Lucius Belton feel wonderful when he saw it in the local newspaper. And when Koko asked him how he had spent his time in Belton, PA, he could answer—with pictorial evidence—"Going to libraries and art galleries."

The librarian-type took a long time to focus his camera, then handed Mrs. Belton the pair of scissors. She snapped them together in the air a few times, as if threatening an invisible butterfly, then said in a soft, cool voice:

"It is a great pleasure, on behalf of my husband, my son and myself, to dedicate this new art gallery for the people of our wonderful town." As the flash bulb went off, she snipped the ribbon with one fast cut.

Digger led the applause. "Hear, hear," he called out.

Mrs. Belton glanced at him and Digger redoubled his efforts. "Brava, brava," he called.

The librarian pushed open the double doors and Mrs. Belton led the group inside a large, simple room with plenty of light from windows on two sides. The walls were filled with expensive-looking oil paintings.

The eight women oohed and aahed a lot as they followed Mrs.

Belton, who walked casually around, looking at the paintings wistfully, as if saying good-bye to old family retainers who were retiring to the county poorhouse. The librarian interrupted: "There is punch and finger sandwiches for everyone over here on this table." The eight women headed for the table as if it contained male pheromones and they were in heat.

This left Mrs. Belton standing in front of a painting, along with Digger. The painting was a large oil landscape, and while Digger did not know the painter, he recognized the school of art as predating the French Impressionists. Mrs. Belton looked at the painting for long seconds, then glanced behind her and noticed Digger.

He nodded toward the painting and affected a French accent.

"An amusing little painting and yet somehow significant, capturing as it does the tortured ambitions of a tumultuous age."

She looked at him, then at the painting again and then back at him.

"You really think so?"

"*Mais oui*, Madame Belton." He pronounced it Belle-TONE.

"Are you an art critic?"

"No, madame. Just a poor itinerant lover of beauty. Le Comte Henri Marie Raymond de Toulouse-Lautrec Monfa at your service." He leaned closer and dropped the accent as he whispered, "I wash and simonize cars for a living. You interested?"

She smiled a real smile, not ceremonial or forced. "Oh, too bad. You're not really Toulouse-Lautrec?"

"No, ma'am. I tried but I failed the physical. Would you like some punch?"

"No, thank you. I've tasted it."

"I'm glad you warned me off," Digger said.

"What *is* your name, by the way?" she asked.

"Sudden," he said. "Oliver. But my friends call me O. L. O. L. Sudden."

"Are you from Belton?" She asked her questions simply and up front, a trait Digger always associated with the rich and the powerful, who gave no thought to the possibility that some persons might find their bluntness offensive.

"No. I'm from Las Vegas," Digger said.

"You're far from home," she said.

"Yes. I'm in town visiting friends. You know, I couldn't help admiring your car. Armor-plated, isn't it?"

She nodded. "My husband's idea. We just had a son and…" She shrugged as if that answered the question thoroughly.

"You look wonderful for a new mamma," Digger said honestly.

"Thank you, Mr. Sudden," she said. "Six months new."

"O. L.," Digger said.

"Yes. Thank you, O. L. I've been to Las Vegas."

"Did you like it?" he said.

"It's wonderful," she said. "The idea of a city that's open all night, every night; it…well, it's quite a contrast to Belton." She seemed to remember then that she was the town's matriarch because she said, "Of course, I don't know if I could really *live* in Las Vegas. The sweetness of this town is probably more my style." She glanced at her watch. "My husband was supposed to be here. I guess he's been detained."

"Your husband is Lucius Belton?" Digger asked.

"Yes."

"My friend used to work for him," Digger said.

"Oh, really," she said without real interest.

"Yes. Perhaps you knew him. Vernon Gillette."

He had watched her face carefully and he could see it freeze over as he mentioned Gillette's name.

"Gillette?" she said. "I can't really place the name. I've got to be going, I'm afraid, Mr. Sudden." She smiled sadly.

"O. L.," Digger corrected.

"Yes, of course. O. L.," she said. "I've got to leave."

"I'm sorry," Digger said. "I was going to offer to buy you coffee."

"I'm afraid I couldn't do that. Perhaps sometime if we meet in Las Vegas," she said.

"I'd like that. You can find me most nights at the Araby Casino," he said.

"I'll keep that in mind," she said.

"Please do," Digger said.

"Well, good-bye," she said. "It was a pleasure meeting you, Mr. Sudden."

"O. L.," Digger said.

Chapter Thirteen

There were no messages for Digger at Gus LaGrande's Inn.

There was no answer when he called Louise Gillette's home.

He found Cody Lord's number in a phone book and called. But an old woman told him that Lord had gone out, and, no, she did not know how Digger might find the Belton hunting cabin in the woods.

Eddie's Roadhouse bar was a madhouse. A Pittsburgh Pirates baseball game was on the tube, and the guys at the bar, all wearing their goddamn cowboy hats, were whooping it up as if they had just been granted weekend leave from prison and were grimly determined to enjoy everything before they had to go back. They shouted at every pitch. They would have cheered a tornado.

Digger sat at a small table by the window. After a few minutes, Dolly saw him and strutted over to the table. Watching her walk across the room seemed to give the bar patrons something else to shout about.

"Hi, stranger," she said to Digger with a smile. The platinum wig and the beauty mark and the push-up bra were back. The makeup was troweled on. She looked nothing like the woman he had made love to two nights before.

"Hiya."

"I was hoping I'd see you again." She leaned forward, showing him her cleavage as if it were an old friend.

"After these coyotes, even I've got to be an improvement," Digger said.

"Yeah, but I need them too. Don't forget the rent. What can I get you?"

"The usual—vodka, rocks, a lot of one, a little of the other."

"Okay. Listen, I'm due a break in ten minutes."

"I'll be here," Digger said.

She came back a few minutes later with his drink, and ten minutes later, returned with another one. "Let's go back in the kitchen," she said. "It's not good for me to sit out here with the customers. It gives these birdbrains ideas."

He followed her into a surprisingly large kitchen, run by one greasy-haired young man wearing a sweat-matted T-shirt. Digger glanced at him and was glad he had never eaten at Eddie's.

Dolly led him to a small table in a far corner, near the freezer door, then poured herself coffee from a big stainless steel urn.

"Just in the neighborhood, thought I'd stop by," Digger said.

"I kind of figured you were leaving town right away, after the other night."

"Everybody seems to want me to," Digger said.

"Oh, how's that?"

"Not important. I guess my charm just doesn't work on people in Belton. Hey, you know, we were talking about that death up in the Belton hunting cabin?" Digger touched the inside of her wrist and toyed with the strap on her watch.

"Yeah," she said. "The accident or not-accident?"

"That's right. You have any idea where that cabin is?"

"Sure," she said brightly. "A lot of the guys from Belton and Sons come in here. I hear them talking. I've had a few invitations."

Digger said, "Tell me how to get there."

"You going up there? Now?"

"Yeah. I thought I ought to see the scene of the crime. Or noncrime."

Dolly gave him clear, simple instructions. The cabin was about fifteen minutes away. Digger finished his drink and waited for Dolly to finish her coffee. As he looked at her, he noticed that under her makeup there was a slight discoloration around her left eye. She glanced at her watch and said, "Back to the lions' den. See you before you leave town?"

"I hope so," Digger said.

"Maybe tonight at Gus's," she said.

He nodded and said, "Call me first. In case I get jammed up with work." He pressed a twenty-dollar bill into her hand. "For the drinks. And the directions."

"Thanks," she said. "Let me go out first. You wait a few minutes. It's not good for us to be seen together. It makes the animals drool."

Dolly's directions were right on the money, and a dozen minutes later Digger was turning off the main road onto one of a string of parallel roads that headed up into the woods, then dipped down toward a random smattering of cabins that fronted a large lake.

Digger was a little disappointed when he first saw the cabin at the end of the road. With Lucius Belton's money, a hunting lodge was the least he had expected, but this cabin was just a cabin. It was built of roughhewn pine. There was no decorative shrubbery around it and no pavement leading to the front door. A television antenna perched on the cabin's flat roof like a giant mosquito with several legs ripped off.

About ten yards before the cabin, a clearing had been cut into the trees off to the left, large enough to hold two cars, so Digger backed in and parked there. The cabin's front door was locked, but Digger twisted the handle and pushed hard and the lock slipped and the door slid open. It might only be a cabin, but it was a good cabin. There was a fireplace, auxiliary electric heaters built in as baseboards, two cots arranged in an L along a far wall, picture windows that overlooked the lake, a couch, a small kitchen area with a table and chairs for two and a television set.

The cabin was clean. Both beds were made. There were no dirty dishes and in the refrigerator were only a few cans of evaporated milk, soup and chili. Digger described the cabin into his tape recorder as he walked around the large single-room interior:

"The bathroom in the corner. Toilet, sink, metal stall shower. Blue-and-white goose shower curtain. Who designs that shit? There it is, the fuse box on the wall. Ooooops, what ho, what ho, what ho! The box has got circuit breakers in it. Two neat little on-off switches for two electrical circuits. Maybe Vernon Gillette wasn't the electrical genius his wife makes him out to be, but you don't have to be an electrical genius to know you don't put fuses into a circuit-breaker box. A chart on the back of the box's cover. 'Installed, Boffa Electric Supplies, 6/76.' A list of inspection dates. June every year: 6/77, 6/78, 6/79, 6/80, 6/81."

Digger closed the circuit-breaker box and walked out of the bathroom. His foot caught on a small throw rug on the floor in the L made by the two cots. On the wooden floor under the rug were two small burn marks. He bent down to look at them, then tried to turn on the lamp on the table between the beds. It didn't work.

"Swell. A lamp without an electric cord. Each burn mark about two inches long, roughly parallel, about a foot apart. They look as if two cigarettes had been placed on the floor and allowed to burn out. I used to get these same kinds of marks all over my desk. When I had a desk. In my previous life."

He stood up and pushed the rug back over the burn marks. As he walked toward the front door, he glanced out the picture window toward the gray lake, looking slatelike and rock-hard in the afternoon sun.

He was preoccupied with his thoughts as he went out the front door. Something slammed into the wall next to him, a fraction of a second before he heard the crack of a shot.

Then there was another. *Thud-crack* and Digger hit the ground and began scrambling for the cover of his car.

"Kwash, you're going to pay for this," he mumbled. He crawled toward the car door. He felt the knee of his pants tear and then the right elbow on his jacket went. Cursing in a steady stream, he reached up from the ground and opened the car door. He heard another shot and dirt kicked up alongside him. Whoever it was was getting the range.

He reached in and pressed the gas pedal with his hand, then released it and turned the ignition key. The motor gunned to life and Digger slipped into the car, keeping his head low. He slammed the car into drive, pressed the gas pedal, spun the wheel to the right and sped off down the dirt road. The rapid acceleration slammed the open driver's door shut.

He started to look up, over the dashboard, when a bullet pierced his rear window.

"Goddammit," he shouted. But it was either a bullet or get wrapped around a tree. He peered warily over the dashboard at the rutted dirt road. Then he made a small turn that he hoped would have him out of the sniper's line of fire and he sat up in the seat.

A moment later, he was back on the main road and he crushed down the gas pedal and sped down the highway, back toward Belton.

He sucked in, then exhaled, a deep sighing breath, and checked the rearview mirror. No one was following him and the road was empty ahead, but it was three more minutes before Digger lightened his foot on the gas pedal and began to drive at safe speeds.

"Goddamn all these Pittsburgh-area half-wit, cowboy, shit-kicker types, goddamn them to hell," he growled.

"A couple of messages for you," Gus said when Digger came into the LaGrande. "What the hell happened to you?"

"Don't ask. What are the messages?"

Gus handed him two slips of paper and Digger read them walking up the steps to his room.

One was from Cody Lord and left his telephone number. The other was from Koko—a typical Koko message. It read: "Where the hell have you been? Call Koko."

From his closet he fished a pair of pants and a clean, unripped jacket. While he sat back on the bed, wriggling out of one pair of pants and into another, he called Koko's number.

"This is Digger. Do you remember me?"

"Not too well. Are you the funny-looking blond thing?" she said.

"Some might say that."

"Where the hell have you been, you blue-eyed devil?"

"Oh, I see," Digger said.

"You see what?"

"You've screwed Hector Blackenbluer into oblivion and now you want to start on me."

"Bullshit, you jealous asshole. I've been calling and calling."

"I only got one message."

"Of course you only got one message," she said. "Nobody ever answers the phone. What the hell kind of place is that anyway?"

"It specializes in teeny-boppers on senior proms who want to orgy. Most of them aren't into telephones."

"You're in a fine mood," she said.

"I ripped my good jacket," he said.

"What good jacket? All your jackets look like fruit-store awnings. Why are you grunting?"

"I'm trying to squirm into a fresh pair of pants," he said.

"I knew you'd find a reason to get your pants off if I left you alone for a couple of days."

"How's your sister?"

"She's okay. They decided not to operate," Koko said.

"I called you a lot," Digger said. "No answer."

"We were running around a lot. We just couldn't connect," she said.

"Sounds like our life story," Digger said.

"How's it by you? How do you like being a goodwill ambassador for BSLI?"

"This is all bullshit, this job," Digger said. "Today I met some guy who looked like a diseased devil and his wife, who looked like an angel. I opened up an art gallery and I got my ass shot at and I ripped my pants and my jacket. I don't need this. I was doing just fine being a degenerate gambler."

"Shot at?" Koko's voice suddenly lost its tone of good humor. "What happened, Dig?"

"I don't know. I was up at the cabin where this Gillette died, trying to look around. And when I left, somebody fired at me."

"Is it hunting country? Maybe some asshole hunter who fires at anything that moves?" she suggested.

"No, it won't wash," Digger said. "Not when they fired a hundred fifty shots at me or put a bullet through my car window while I was getting my butt out of there. I miss you."

"I miss you too, Dig. Is that an invitation?"

Digger propped the phone between shoulder and ear and zipped up his fly. He looked up at the red pendant on the crystal chandelier.

"Yeah, it's an invitation," he said. "This was going to be our pleasant weekend together. Now the weekend's almost shot and me too."

"Is it an invitation or not an invitation?"

"Invitation," he said.

"Okay. I'll be there tonight," Koko said.

"Hold on. How you getting here?"

"I'll take a bus to Belton and then I'll call you to pick me up. If you're not there, I'll get a cab. Don't worry. I'm really very self-sufficient."

"I know that."

"I'll be there tonight. What are you going to do now?"

"I'm going to try to find out who shot at me."

"Digger, be careful. Was this a murder?"

"Yeah. I'm sure of it now."

"Then they won't mind killing you. Be careful."

"I will. You just get your ass here rickety-sprit."

Koko giggled. "I'm on my way. Have them warm up a horse for me."

"What horse?" Digger said. "What are you talking about?"

"I'm talking about that herd of lalapaloozas out your front window—what do you think I'm talking about?" She paused. "You lied, didn't you?"

"To hell with them. I'll buy you your own pony."

"I hate you, Digger."

"Come anyway," he said. "I need protection."

Digger put on his jacket and called Cody Lord's number.

"This is Burroughs," he said.

"Oh, yeah. I'm sorry I missed you before."

"I bet you are," Digger said. "I want to talk to you. Where do you live?"

Lord gave him an address and Digger said, "Where do I find it?"

"Just come down Church Street to the big tire store. Turn right there. I'm on the next corner."

"I'll be right there."

The red pickup truck was parked in front of Cody Lord's house, and as Digger walked by it, he put his hand on the hood. It was warm.

Even before the echo of the doorbell had died out, Lord opened the door.

"Come on in, Mr. Burroughs," he said and waved Digger into a small, sparsely furnished living room. "Can I get you a drink?"

"You have vodka?"

"Yes."

"On the rocks," Digger said. As Lord left the room, Digger looked around, and his attention was drawn to a large gun cabinet in a far corner of the room. It held three rifles, and under them were four trophies. Digger looked at them; they were for target shooting in rifle competition.

Lord was back in a minute with a large water glass filled with ice and vodka. Digger remembered that Lord had not even sipped his beer that day in Eddie's. He would be a nondrinker. Nondrinkers always made drinks with nine times as much liquor in them as they should have. They didn't appreciate the ritualistic aspects of refilling one's glass.

Lord popped the top of a can of Coke and sipped from it as he sat down in a chair facing Digger.

"Where were you today?" Digger asked.

Lord shrugged. "I'm sorry, I must have just missed you when you called. I was out getting my car lubed. My mother told me that you called. She doesn't live here, but she stops in once in a while just to make sure I'm all right. Her little boy, you know."

"And since then?" Digger asked.

"Nowhere. I've been home all day."

Digger let the lie pass.

"I drove out to the cabin that you and Gillette used."

"Oh, yeah. Ma told me. Did you find out anything?"

"Yeah," Digger said. "That somebody wants to kill me."

"What?" Lord said, sitting forward in his chair.

"You heard me. Somebody pegged some shots at me."

"Jesus," Lord said. He paused for a moment, as if thinking. "Damn it, that proves it, doesn't it? That somebody killed Vern?"

"Yeah," Digger said. "Somebody."

Cody Lord seemed to wilt under his gaze. "Hey," he said weakly, "wait a minute. Vern was my friend. You can't think—"

"I'll tell you what I think," Digger said. "I think you think I'm awfully stupid."

"What?" Lord's voice was a whine, trying to understand.

"Why'd you call me the other night and drop a dime on the Orleans jazz club?"

"Oh. I...well, I thought you might find something out there about Vern's death."

"You knew he was banging the singer," Digger said.

"I...I wasn't sure."

"You're a liar," Digger said. "You sent me there without telling me it was you. What the hell did you think I was going to do? Have a drink, listen to those lunatics butcher 'Perdido,' then go home? You knew about the singer."

"Okay. I'm sorry about that, Mr. Burroughs. I knew Vern was having an affair with some singer there. I just didn't want to say anything bad about him."

"Bad? What's bad? Maybe what's bad is if Gillette's wife is giving some out on the side to his best friend."

Lord bristled. "I resent that. Louise is a fine—"

"And I don't give a damn what you resent. What I know is that somebody killed Gillette. You keep saying he was your best friend, but I think you've been having an affair with his wife. I think you've been lying to me from the start and today's the biggest lie of all."

"What do you mean?"

"You were home all day?"

"Yes."

"Why is your truck's motor still warm?" Digger asked. "Let me give you a clue. You found out I was going up to that cabin and you sneaked up there and gave me a real warm Belton, PA, welcome. And then you hustled back here. How's that sound?"

Lord shook his head from side to side. "No, no, no," he said. His shoulders slumped and he sank down in his chair.

"I'll tell you what happened," he said.

"Don't leave anything out this time," Digger said.

"I won't. Vern *was* my best friend. And, yeah, you're right, I was in love with his wife anyway. But I wouldn't do anything about it, Mr. Burroughs, 'cause I don't believe in that. Anyway, I knew he was cheating on Louise. I know this is terrible, but when he died, well, sure I was sad, but I thought then that I had a chance with Louise. But she's so wrapped up in Vern's memory that there's no space in her head for me."

"There's enough space in her head for everybody," Digger said. "Go ahead."

"I really think Vern was killed, Mr. Burroughs. I don't know why or who. Louise never wanted to believe that. When you came to town, I thought you could get at the truth. And I thought that it might help you if you knew where Vern hung out. I don't know...I thought if you found out about the singer and if you told Louise about it, then it might free her from Vern's memory and I would have a chance. If *I* told her that he cheated, she'd hate me. That's why I did it the way I did, Mr. Burroughs."

"You weren't up that cabin just now? Why was your motor warm?" Digger asked.

"I was over to see Louise. She called and asked me to come over." He got up and went to the phone. "She wants to talk to you."

"About what?" Digger asked as Lord dialed the phone.

"About the insurance money," Lord said. Into the phone, he said, "Louise, Mr. Burroughs is here." He nodded and said, "Wait a moment." He asked Digger, "Can you go over and see her now? She wants to talk to you."

"Yes," Digger said.

"He'll be right over," Lord said. "Okay. 'Bye, Louise."

Digger drained his drink and got to his feet as Lord hung up. "One thing," he said. "I called Louise's today. There wasn't any answer. About two-forty. You were there then?"

Lord blushed. "The next time you're screwing your best friend's widow," Digger said, "take the phone off the hook. Don't just ignore it. It makes people wonder."

Lord nodded.

"The night you left Vern at the cabin? You went to see Louise, didn't you?" Digger asked.

"Yes. I asked her to leave Vern and marry me. She said no."

"When you met her here that first day," Digger said, "did you tell anybody about it?"

Lord said, "No. Just Louise."

"And who did you tell today that I was going up the cabin?" Digger asked.

"Just Louise," Lord said.

"Who do you think killed Vern Gillette?" Digger asked.

"I don't know. I didn't. Really. And I didn't have anything to do with shooting at you today, Mr. Burroughs. Honest, I didn't."

"I know that," Digger said as he opened the door. "You don't have the balls."

Chapter Fourteen

"Hello, Ardath. How's my favorite doorman?"

"Hello, Mr. Burroughs. Come in, please. My mother's expecting you. She put her trains away." The little girl closed the door behind Digger, then wrapped her hand around his left index and middle finger and pulled him down to her.

"Did you solve our mysterious death yet?" she asked in a whisper.

"No, Ardath, but I'm trying. I'm really trying," he whispered back.

"I "know," she said. "Somehow I have faith that you will succeed where others have failed."

She stood up straight and very formally said, "Come this way, Mr. Burroughs." And she winked at him, a coconspirator with a ponytail.

"Hey, not so fast," Digger whispered. "I've got a question to ask."

"All right."

"The last time I was here, did you let Cody Lord in the house?"

"No. Cody lets himself in, usually by the back kitchen door. He has the run of the house." She looked around and moved closer to Digger's ear. "He's around a lot these days. I think he is infatuated with my mother."

A muffled voice called out. "Ardath? Who's there?"

The little girl pulled Digger down the hall. "Coming, Mother," she called.

Louise Gillette was in a small sitting room across from her Grand Central Station. She was sipping a Bloody Mary. She wore a tight halter and shorts cut so high they barely encroached upon her thighs. Her midriff, tight and unfleshed, was bare, and her dark hair was tousled about her head. There was a pleased, satisfied look in her eyes, and Digger thought that Cody Lord might be a simp but he certainly knew how to service Louise Gillette's account.

"Mr. Burroughs," she said.

"Lord said you wanted to see me."

"Yes. Ardath, you can leave us alone now."

"Yes, Mother. Call if you need anything."

"Thank you, I will."

After Ardath had closed the door behind her, Louise Gillette invited Digger to sit down, and he flopped into a chair facing hers across a wooden cocktail table.

"I've decided to take your company's offer of a million dollars," she said.

"Why?"

"Is that really important? Doesn't it suffice that I am relieving BSLI of its major headache by agreeing to terms? Not saying anything, of course, about what it will do for your reputation at your company. To bring me back on your shield, so to speak."

She sipped at her drink and looked over the rim of the glass at him with satisfied eyes. Or maybe they were just smug, Digger thought.

"Well, to take your points in no particular order, Mrs. Gillette. Yes, my company would be happy to be relieved of a headache and you have been a headache. Next, as for my reputation with the company, my reputation is zip code with everybody except one person at the company, and I don't care at all about my reputation because, frankly, I'm used to doing my job correctly, which is very rare at Old Benevolent and Saintly, which is built upon a rock-solid foundation of failure. Next, yes, it is really important that I know why you decided to take the million dollars."

"An additional five hundred thousand dollars is a lot of money," she said blandly.

"And it was just as much money three months ago when my company first sent its envoys to talk to you, those people with the teeth. Maybe it was even more money then, counting for inflation. Let's see, adjusting for an annual rate of twelve percent, in three months you've lost three percent of five hundred thousand, and that is…is…a lot of money."

"I've just decided that it seems senseless to deprive Ardath of such a financial start in life, just over some arbitrary principle," she said.

"I think it was in the train station across the hall, Mrs. Gillette, that someone told me that principles aren't worth anything unless they *are* arbitrary."

"Times change. People change."

"Often suddenly," Digger said, "and not generally without reason."

"Listen, Mr. Burroughs. I didn't ask you here to spar with you intellectually. I asked you here to tell you my decision. 'Tell.' That's the important part of that sentence. Not to discuss or ask your advice. To tell you my decision."

"Have you ever been to the cabin where your husband died?"

"No. The police wouldn't let anybody up there at first, and then, afterwards, well, I didn't ever want to see that place."

"Your husband died changing a fuse, isn't that correct?"

"That's what the police said."

"And that's what you'll be saying if you decide you want the million dollars?" Digger said.

"I guess so," she said, almost reluctantly, as if she had not until then realized the impact of what she was doing. She put down her glass and nervously began turning it on the coaster on the table.

"Initially," Digger said, "you were concerned that your subscribing to that cause of death would make you an accomplice in stating that your husband was a fool?"

"Yes. That's about right," she said.

"Well, if you believe that now, Mrs. Gillette, your husband was no fool. Your husband was a flaming idiot."

"That's rude, crude and uncalled-for," she snapped.

"I'll tell you how your husband died changing a fuse," Digger said. The woman was silent, staring angrily at him.

"There wasn't any goddamn fuse box in that cabin. It had circuit breakers. Now maybe all you geniuses practice a different form of electricity with your toy subways and all your bullshit, but when I grew up, I knew you don't put fuses in circuit-breaker boxes."

She slumped back in her chair. "What you're saying..."

"What I'm saying is that I'm pretty sure your husband was murdered. What price do you put on his life, Mrs. Gillette? You want to take your extra five hundred thou and run away and let his killer escape? Is that what you're telling me to do?"

The woman was silent, but her lips were working as if she were talking to herself and only by great effort preventing her words from spewing forth into the room. Finally, she said, "I want to think about things, Mr. Burroughs."

"I'd still like to know who or what convinced you to change your mind about the money," Digger said.

"I told you, I'd like to think about this for a while. I'll be in touch."

Digger looked over toward this bookshelf. Another college photograph of Vern Gillette—athlete, scholar, husband, father, genius and murder victim—seemed to be staring at him.

"Call me," Digger told the woman. "I'm at Gus's LaGrande Inn."

"I know. Cody told me."

"Yes. I'm sure he did."

As Digger slid behind the wheel of his car, he saw Ardath sitting in the front passenger seat.

"Ah, good, you've decided to run away with me," he said.

"No. I wanted to talk to you," she said very seriously. "What happened to your rear window?"

"Vandalism," Digger said. There was no need to frighten the girl.

She nodded slowly as if trying to make up her mind whether or not to believe him.

"Do you think my father was murdered?"

"Yes."

"By whom?"

"I don't know," Digger said. "Not yet."

"Will you be able to find out?" she asked.

"I absolutely guarantee it," he said. "Count on it."

"Good," she said. "I'll run along now. I know you must be busy."

"A few small questions first," Digger said.

"Are these connected with our case?" she asked.

Our case? Yes, Digger agreed silently, it was their case.

"Yes," he said. "Do you know who telephoned your mother today?"

"There was one call, but she was sitting by the telephone and answered it first, so I don't know who called."

"Did you hear any of the conversation?"

"No. I was in another room. After Mother was on the phone, Cody came over."

"Do you think she might have been talking to him on the phone?"

"I really don't know. They made love when he came over."

"What?" Digger said.

"Really, Mr. Burroughs. After all, I'm eight. They made love."

"How can you be sure?"

"My mother sent me over to my friend Wilma's to play. Wilma is an idiot and my mother knows it. She only sends me there when she wants to make love to Cody."

"Does that happen often?" Digger asked.

"Not...oh, I see. You want to know if they made love before my father died."

"I was getting to that."

"No, Mr. Burroughs, I'm quite sure of it. Never before Daddy died. Only recently they became lovers."

"How do you feel about that?" Digger asked.

"It's my mother's decision actually. He's not really the type of man I would choose for anybody, especially myself. He's wishy-washy."

"My feelings exactly."

"I don't think he killed my father," she said.

"Neither do I," Digger said.

They were silent a moment, then Ardath asked, "Do you have children?"

"Yes. Two. What's-his-name and the girl."

"They're very lucky to have you as a father," she said.

"If that's so, why do they have my picture posted in their kitchen with a five-hundred-dollar reward sign on it?" Digger asked.

"They don't understand you. You should try talking to them."

"How?" Digger asked. "How can I talk to them? They're not dolphins."

She smiled and started to get out of the car. "I'll leave now," she said. Standing at the side of the car, she said, "I almost forgot, Mr. Burroughs. A police car drove by and the policeman stopped and stared at your car."

"Did he see you?" Digger asked.

"He must have, but no one notices children. He just stared."

"Was he a big guy with a face that looks like it's mutating into a hogshead?"

She giggled, an eight-year-old's giggle.

"A very good description," she said. "That was him. There was a lady with him."

"What did she look like?"

"I didn't really see. A blond lady, though."

Walter Brackler's home phone did not answer, so Digger called Frank Stevens, the president of BSLI.

Stevens's big, bluff voice seemed to echo through the phone.

"Ah, Digger. The playboy of the western world. How are you?"

"All right, Frank."

"Brackler told me that you think you might have a murder on your hands. He seemed annoyed that you were complicating things."

"That's right," Digger said. "It's a murder. Someone even pegged some shots at me today."

"Who?" Stevens said.

"I don't know yet. Does Brackler have an alibi?"

"He's not the violent type," Stevens said.

"Keep an eye on him," Digger said. "I'm going to be staying here a little while."

Chapter Fifteen

DIGGER'S LOG:

Tape Recording Number Four, 6:30 P.M., Saturday, Julian Burroughs in the matter of Vernon Gillette.

Listen up, Rosicrucians. Pay attention, Scientologists, Moonies, Holly-Gollies, transcendental meditators, you're all wrong.

All the wisdom of the universe can be summed up in three mighty iron-clad principles which never waver. Governments come and go; new religions flourish, then die; but these three principles are absolutes.

One. I am not in this business to get shot at.

Two. Getting shot at sucks.

Three. When I find out who shot at me, I will express my unhappiness in the strongest possible terms. Except if he's still shooting at me, in which case I'll take off like a big-ass bird.

There are three new tapes in the master file. The first involved my descent into the inferno today to meet The Old Man, Lucius Belton. I wouldn't say he's infirm, but he's not firm either, and there is an evil glitter to his eyes. "How art thou fallen from heaven, Oh Lucifer, son of the morning!" Isaiah 14:12. See, world. Aren't you proud that I learned to read the Bible in three languages—English for my father, Hebrew for my mother and Latin for my Jesuit professors at St. Luke's. I want my tombstone suitably inscribed.

Anyway, old Lucifer knew I was coming, and his people knew my license number, courtesy, I'm sure, of the local gendarmerie. I didn't like Belton as soon as I saw his bare office walls. Bare walls intimidate you because you know the bastard who occupies that office has done away with all frippery and when he's looking at you, you know he thinks you're just more frippery to do away with. In fact, he kind of offered to do away with me unless I behaved.

Belton hasn't spoken to Louise Gillette since the funeral, at least as of 12:30 today. But he knew Gillette died in an accident. He just knew it. It had to be an accident. Pay the lady the million and please leave town.

Yes, indeedy, Vern Gillette was his friend and successor-to-be at Belton and Sons. The big policy was just a fringe in case anything happened to him. As something did. Belton, with his blue oxygen-starved fingers, is a consummate liar, but at least he admitted that his relationship with Gillette had cooled. Something about Louise and Amanda not getting along. Do I believe that? Sure. Almost as much as I believe in the Easter bunny.

Tape Two is Mrs. Belton, lovely Amanda, who arrived at the library in her armored personnel carrier, cut a ribbon and chatted with me until I mentioned Gillette's name and then denied knowing the man and fled. Poor woman. If she gets bored cutting ribbons at libraries, what must it be like at home at night with Lucifer, the Walking Dead. My picture's going to be in the paper with her, shouting Brava at the ribbon cutting. I hope Belton sees it. That'll teach him to threaten me. Let's see. I didn't get Dolly on tape when she gave me directions and I've got to be careful 'cause she might call me tonight and I don't want her to do that if Koko's here. I'll tell Gus not to put through any calls.

And then up to the hunting lodge on Tape Two and home away from home for Vern Gillette. No fuses in the cabin. Circuit breakers. So much for an accident changing a fuse. I don't get those two little burn marks on the floor near the bed. Anyway, I got four shots fired at me. By whom? I don't know. Cody Lord was the only person who knew I was going up there, but I don't figure him for the killer even though he's nuts about Gillette's wife and he's banging her. Anyway, I saw his rifle trophies. If he wanted to put me away, he wouldn't have missed. I lucked up because whoever was shooting at me was using a pistol.

Louise Gillette knew I was going up there because Lord told her. But he told her while they were in bed making love—I can recognize the signs—and anyway, if she wanted to kill her husband, she'd be too smart to do it with electric fuses in a cabin that doesn't use fuses.

Hold that. Cody and Louise weren't the only two who knew I was going up to the cabin. Dolly Knockers knew too. But she doesn't look like the rapid-fire shooter type. More like one bang at a time.

Wait until the car-rental company sees the nice shattered windshield in the back of their car. Have fun, Kwash. Explain that one away.

Tape Three, we've got Cody Lord and Louise, and Lord makes sense. He sent me to the Orleans because he wanted me to carry back the stories about his dead buddy sleeping around. Damn it, he's got motive. He left Gillette up at the cabin and came down to seduce Gillette's wife. They cook up a scheme and Lord goes back and figures out a way to electrocute him, and then makes believe he finds the body the next day. Then he and Louise live happily ever after on the insurance money.

Except if that held water, why did she initially turn down the million? Why get me involved investigating things? And who could believe Lord killing anybody? Not me.

Then Louise Gillette, telling me she changed her mind about the million, that closes Tape Three. Why'd she change her mind? Count on it. The Devil made her do it. Lucifer Belton. I don't think she knows she only gets a half million in a murder. I'm not going to tell her. Leave that pleasant duty to Kwash when the time comes.

And Tape Three ends with my visit with Ardath Gillette, the only person in this town that I respect and trust. She just confirmed a lot of stuff and also told me that a cop came by to look at my car. Deputy Harker by the looks of him. With a blond woman. Hanging out with Harker, she must be a real beaut.

All right, I've gone through all of this and I still don't know anything. I'll just chew it around some more. Where the hell is Koko? She's good at stuff like this.

All right, expenses. Thirty dollars for gas. I've been driving all over this place and Belton, PA, is bigger than Canada. Eight dollars for lunch with Mrs. Pfoopler; two dollars for newspapers; ten dollars for a donation to the new town art gallery; forty dollars for drinks with Dolly, who gave me directions to the cabin. That's ninety dollars. I am not paying for the repairs to that rental-car window. Also, company, you are paying for a new jacket and pants for me, but I don't know how much yet until my Savile Row tailor gives me an estimate. The items may just be irreplaceable, in which case you'll pay even more.

I'm going downstairs and wait for Koko.

Chapter Sixteen

"Hey, check this out," Gus LaGrande whispered to Digger. The inn's owner was looking toward the entrance hallway at a delicate young woman who had paused at the entrance to the bar. She was wearing a brown silk blouse, tucked into men's-style jeans rolled up into cuffs to show off hand-tooled leather boots. A wide leather belt with a saucer-sized silver buckle nipped in tight around her tiny waist. Long black hair framed a face that was all delicately exotic sloe eyes and salad oil-smooth skin. She wore a chocolate-brown stetson pushed back on her head, and it made her small, perfect features seem even tinier.

"Ten bucks says I can get over on her," Digger said.

Gus looked at him, at the woman again and said, "You're on."

The woman came into the bar and sat across from Digger. Gus turned to approach her when Digger called out, "Hey, lady."

"What?" she responded. "What do you want, fella?"

"I'll give you two dollars to do disgusting things to my body."

"Cheapskate," she said. "I never take less than four."

"Two-fifty," Digger said.

"Three-fifty."

"Three," Digger said. "Not a penny more."

"Okay," she said. "But you buy the penicillin."

Gus LaGrande's head was tennis-matching back and forth. His mouth hung open as the young woman got up, walked around the bar and threw her arms around Digger's neck. They kissed and Digger said, "Koko, this is Gus. He owes me ten dollars."

"That's a switch. A bartender owing you money," she said. She sat next to Digger and ordered Perrier water.

"Why do you drink that crap?" Digger asked. "It's club soda."

"Sure, it is. But it comes in a bottle. I don't want to drink anything that comes out of a hose in a bar. How do you know what's been in the hose? You taught me that. I just arrived and already you're bitching at me?"

"I'm not bitching. Drink whatever you want. I thought you were going to call me to pick you up."

"There was a cab right near the bus stop and I thought I'd save you the trouble. You don't look too bad."

"Was I supposed to?"

"I don't know. Somebody shot at you, I thought you'd be hiding in a corner under a table."

"The bullet ain't been made with my name on it, little lady," Digger drawled. "Where'd you get that silly cowboy hat?"

"I bought it up at my mother's. I love it."

"It looks nice," Digger said. "It's just that it makes you look like all those other knickknacks around here. Everybody in Belton, PA, wears a cowboy hat."

She whispered in his ear, "Play your cards right, I'll let you rip it off me."

"Hold that thought," he said.

"I'm glad to see you. I got a scare when I was coming up here."

"What was that?" Digger asked.

"A cop's car was parked down near the foot of the drive. I thought maybe you were in some kind of trouble."

"No, I'm not in trouble," he said. "Was there a cop in it?"

"Yes. Some big slug. He looked like a snail in a hat."

"I'm in trouble," Digger said. "I think he's the one that pegged the shots at me. What was he doing?"

"Just sitting there."

"He's waiting for me," Digger whined. "The bastard's waiting for me to take a step out into the street and then he's going to draw down on me and leave my bleeding body in the dust. I hate Belton, PA."

"I don't want you shot at," Koko said. "You're not much, but I don't want you killed before I get you trained."

Digger stared glumly into his drink because he was afraid. Not for himself, but because he didn't want Koko around if anybody made another strafing run at him. Who knew what that bastard Harker was capable of? It was a bad idea letting Koko come here.

"What's wrong, Digger?" she said.

"Who says something's wrong?"

"I've been here five minutes already and you haven't tried to force me into bed yet."

"What do you think I am, some kind of animal?"

"We'll let that pass without comment," she said.

"You sit here and wait a minute."

"Where are you going?"

"Up to my room," Digger said.

"I want to see your room."

"It's haunted," he said.

"What?"

"The presence of Hondle Sycamore permeates the place," Digger said. "I haven't slept since I got here. I feel his cold fingers on my neck."

"Hugo Stockelbrinner," she said. "Don't worry about it. I laughed him off nine years ago, I can do it again." She paused. "He had *warm* fingers as I recall. With warts."

"You wait here."

"I'll accompany you. For protection."

"Boy, you just can't get him out of your mind, can you?" Digger grumbled. "We'll be right back," he told Gus.

She followed Digger into his room, then whirled around, looking at it.

"This is it, Dig. The very room. Even that stupid red pendant is still on the chandelier."

"You're disgusting. All you think about is sex, sex, sex," Digger said.

"Same bed too. I remember the big brass headboard."

"You want me to send downstairs? Maybe they still have the same sheets." Digger was fumbling in a dresser drawer, dumping a pile of tape cassettes into a small plastic laundry bag. When he turned around, he saw that Koko had flopped onto the bed. She extended her arms toward him.

"Same mattress too," she said. "Come here, Dig, I'll relieve your tensions."

"Talk about creatures of habit," he said. "You just don't know how to act once you get in this room."

"Well, maybe it's best," she said. "Maybe the memories of this room ought to belong only to Hugo and me. Dear, sweet Hugo. I wonder what he's doing now. Maybe I'll call and see if he's still around."

Digger growled and dove on top of her. She buried her lips against his and when he finally let her go, she said, "I knew if I was subtle and smart, I'd eventually wear you down. Make love to me."

"In a little while," he said.

"Thanks for the rejection," she said, sitting up.

"It's not a rejection. You'll understand later. Come on."

"Where are we going?"

"Just trust me," Digger said.

"The last man I trusted was Hugo Stockelbrinner. At least he meant well. Actually, though, he did pretty well too."

Downstairs, he had Koko wait in the lobby hall while he talked to Gus in the bar.

"Gus, are you going to be here tonight? Can I borrow your car?"

Gus hesitated a second. "Sure," he said. "Something wrong with yours?"

"It's lugging a little bit," Digger lied. "I don't want to chance it."

"Okay." Gus handed him a set of car keys. "It's the green Volvo to the right of the door."

"Good." Digger took out his wallet and handed Gus a fifty-dollar bill.

"You don't have to do that," Gus said.

"Company expenses," Digger said. He leaned close so that Koko could not overhear. "Listen, remember that girl who was here the other night?"

"Yeah. Dolly? Was that her name?" Gus asked.

"Yes. If she comes in, looking for me, tell her to wait."

"All right."

"And if anybody calls, take messages. I'll be calling in."

"You're quite a man," Gus said.

Digger grunted. "Here's my car keys," he said. "In case you need it."

"Which car is yours?" Gus asked.

"The one with the bullet hole in the back windshield," Digger said.

"Now drive naturally," Digger said. "And keep an eye open and see if the cop's car is still there. Then turn left onto the main road."

"Okay," Koko said.

Digger lay on the back seat as Koko went careening down the narrow road that led from the LaGrande to the main highway.

"Slow down, for Christ's sakes," he yelled.

"You said drive naturally. This is natural."

"Then drive unnaturally slow. I'm going to wet my pants," he said.

Koko slowed down, then stopped at the entrance to the highway.

"Cop's car is still there," she said softly. "The gorilla's still in it."

"Okay. Make your left onto the highway and keep driving."

He felt the car turn left and accelerate smoothly down the road.

"Is he following you?" Digger asked.

"No."

"Good." Digger sat up and peeked out the rear window. There were no cars behind them.

"Okay," he said. "When you get over this hill, pull off and stop. I'll drive."

"Why you? You always get lost," she said.

"Because you drive like a goddamn kamikaze and I'm not ready yet to drive into a battleship's smokestack."

"You're a pain in the ass, Digger."

"Yes, I am. Pull over."

"What is this place?" Koko asked.

"It's a motel. What does it look like?"

"It looks like a goddamn chicken barn," Koko said. "What are we doing here?"

"Just wait here a minute," Digger said as he got out of Gus LaGrande's car.

He was back in a few minutes.

"We're in luck," he said. "It's in the back."

"What's in the back?"

"You'll see."

"If I wanted to stay in rooms like this," Koko said, "I could start turning tricks in Times Square."

"Don't exaggerate. It's not that bad. Look. You've even got a free newspaper, courtesy of the management."

"Not bad, huh? And I bet you can't beat the price either. You know what's wrong with you, Digger?"

"I'm sure you'll tell me," he said.

"You're just like your mother."

"That's a foul accusation," Digger said.

"She buys your father's ties at Tie City and she buys paper plates at Paper City. Your father's shoes come from Shoe City. If she had to have surgery done, she'd have it done at Knife City. Just as long as it's cheap. You're the same way. Look at this place. Motel City. I left my mother's beautiful house to come see you and you want me to stay in this dump."

"It has its charms," Digger said.

"Name one."

"Nobody will shoot at you here," he said.

She looked at him for three long seconds, then draped her arms over his shoulders.

"Oh, Dig. That's what this is all about?"

"Yes, ma'am."

"Oh, Dig."

"I ain't letting you get killed until I get me some Oriental nookie," he said.

"You had to go and spoil a tender moment, didn't you?" she said.

"You know me. Bad Joke City," he said.

He left Koko hunkered down with his tapes and tape recorder and the complimentary motel copy of the *Belton Bulletin*. At a phone booth in a gas station he called Gus LaGrande.

"Any calls?" he asked.

"Yes. Louise called. She wants you to call her. Do you know her? That's the only name she'd give—just Louise."

"Yeah, I know her. No other calls?"

"No. Do you mind if I ask, how many women do you know in this town? Is there any broad you don't know?"

"Women are the custodians of the world's secrets," Digger said. "He who would be wise would cultivate women."

"That's too deep for me."

"Try this," Digger said. "If Dolly with the big tits comes in, hold her there for me."

Digger dialed Louise Gillette's number. When she answered, she wasted no time in pleasantry.

"Mr. Burroughs, I agree with you. I think my husband was murdered."

"Did something happen to change your mind?" he asked.

"I drove up to the campsite with Cody. I looked at the electricity and I saw the bullet holes near the door where somebody shot at you. Until I saw that, I think I believed you were lying."

"I wasn't."

"And then Ardath told me about the window in your car, and how Lem Harker was driving by, looking it over."

"One of the bullets got that," Digger said.

"Mr. Burroughs, I want you to find the killer. I'll retain your services for whatever it costs."

"You're already paying enough," Digger said. "Double indemnity doesn't apply in cases of murder. If we're right, your insurance is only worth five hundred thousand."

"I don't give a damn if it's worth only six cents. I don't need the money. I want my husband's killer."

"All right," Digger said. "Who called you today and convinced you to take the million?"

"Lucius Belton," she said immediately.

"How'd he get you to change your mind?"

"Oh, well," she said with a sigh, "I'm sure you'd find out sooner or later."

"Yes, I would," Digger said.

"He told me any investigation into Vern's death wouldn't turn up anything except the fact that Vern was having affairs with a number of women." She paused a moment. "Belton used me, Mr. Burroughs. He knew how protective I was of Vern's reputation."

"It sounds like it," Digger said.

"I hate being used," she said. "Do you think he had anything to do with Vern's death?"

"I don't know. I don't have a motive for him," Digger said.

"Find out. Mr. Burroughs?"

"Yes."

"Was my husband having an affair?"

"Yes."

"With whom?" she asked.

"Nobody you know," Digger said.

"I'll let that stand for now. If there's anything you want me to do, let me know."

"I will," Digger said.

Marla Manning winked and nodded to Digger when he walked by the piano. When her set was over, she joined him at a small table in the back of the Orleans jazz club.

"Hiya, Walt," she said. "I guess I ought to thank you for getting me across the road last night. I was ripped out of my gourd."

"Right and wrong," he said.

"What do you mean?"

"Right, you were ripped. Wrong. My name's not Walt."

She pushed her chair back a little from the table.

"Oh?"

"No, my name is Julian Burroughs, and I'm in town investigating the murder of Vern Gillette."

"Murder? What…?"

"No, Marla, it won't work," Digger said. "You know more than you've been telling me and that gig's over now. You can tell me and I can clean this up and keep you out of it, or you can let me turn everything over to the state cops and you can tell them all about it."

"What am I supposed to know?" she asked.

"I know you were up in the cabin with Gillette the night he got killed."

"How do you *know* that?" she asked.

The trouble was Digger didn't know. He suspected but he didn't know. He decided to run a bluff. He pushed his chair back and started to his feet.

"Sorry, Marla. We don't have anything more to talk about. You can tell it to the cops."

She leaned forward and grabbed his sleeve.

"Sit down, dammit," she said.

"To listen to more of your bullshit?" he said. "No thanks."

"Sit down. Please."

Digger sat down, but perched on the edge of the chair as if ready to leave as soon as he could.

"Okay, I was up there," she said.

"I know," he said. "Now tell me about it. And don't leave anything out."

"All right. That night. When I got done work here, I drove up. Vern invited me that day. He said he was going to be alone, so I went up."

"And the two of you made it. Then what happened?"

"We went to sleep. There were just those two shaky little cots, so we slept separate. I guess we just fell asleep and we heard a noise like somebody outside. Vern was afraid. He thought it was his wife snooping on him."

"Then what happened?" Digger asked.

"I got my clothes on real fast in the dark and I got out of there," Marla said.

"Did you see anybody?"

"No. We didn't put any lights on so I could get out of there without being seen. Vern walked with me to the car. I cut out and he was going back to the cabin. I don't know." Marla buried her head in her hands. "I don't know. I've thought about it a hundred times since then. I think I heard a voice and then I heard a thud. I'm not sure."

"You didn't stop to see?" Digger said.

"No. Vern wanted me out of there, so I got out of there." She looked up at Digger and said, "That's it. That's all of it."

And he knew she was lying.

"That's not quite all of it," he said.

"What are you talking about?"

He started to rise again. "Tell it to the cops. I've got no time for this crap."

"Sit down," she said. "What'd you say your name was?"

"Julian Burroughs. My friends call me Digger."

"Then you don't hear that name much," she said. "You're a heartless bastard."

"Don't forget it," Digger said.

"All right. There was one other thing."

"I'm waiting," he said.

"I raced like hell down to the bottom of that road to get out of there. When I turned the corner, I saw a cop's car parked alongside the main road. I was scared now and worried about Vern. I didn't know what to do, but I stopped my car and I walked over to the cop's car."

"And there wasn't anybody in it," Digger said.

"How did you know?" she asked.

"Never mind. Then what'd you do?"

"I went home. I didn't hear anything until I read in Monday's paper that Vern died."

"And you didn't tell the cops?" Digger asked.

"What was to tell? I didn't see anything. I didn't really know anything."

"You saw the cop's car," Digger reminded her.

"What does that mean? It didn't mean anything. Maybe he had a flat. I didn't stay around long enough to find out. Maybe he was taking a leak in the woods."

"And you just let it go at that?" Digger said.

"Yes. Would you have done differently?"

"I don't know," Digger said.

She paused and said, "Was Vern really murdered?"

"Yes," he said.

"By a cop?"

"I don't know. Think back. When you were in the cabin, was there a rug on the floor between the beds?"

"A rug. I don't know."

"Think," he said. "When you got out of bed in a hurry, were your feet cold from the floor? Were you standing on a rug?"

She thought. "No," she said finally, "there wasn't any rug. Is that important?"

"It is to me. I do home decorating on the side. Maybe I can sell them some rugs for the cabin."

"You're not funny."

"Try this," Digger said. "Did the lamp in the cabin work? The little one between the beds?"

"Yes. What's that about?"

"You don't need to know," Digger said.

"You know," she said, "I really loved Vern."

"It didn't help him much. He's still dead and his killer's still loose."

"You're a bastard," she said.

"Only to my friends."

The police car was gone from the entrance to Gus's LaGrande when Digger turned up the long curving driveway to the inn. Dolly smiled at him when she saw him walk into the bar. She was still wearing a little heavier makeup to cover the bruise near her left eye, but with her medium-brown hair she looked half a world away from the platinum sexpot who waited tables at Eddie's.

He sat next to her and she was happy to see him; she had thought she might not see him again and that would have been awful, and how was his day?

"I've had better," Digger said. Without being asked, Gus put vodka on the bar in front of him and nodded a conspirator's greeting.

"Listen, Dolly," Digger said, "let's take our drinks with us. I've got something to show you upstairs."

She whispered in his ear, "I hope so."

In his room they sat at the small dining table.

"Let's talk," he said.

"I was hoping you had something else in mind," she said.

"Really talk," Digger said coldly. Something in his voice must have startled her because she said, "I don't know if I like you like this."

"I get worse. Something about being shot at sours my disposition."

"Shot at?" The surprise in her eyes was genuine, Digger thought.

"Today. Up at the cabin. Somebody tried to make me into wallpaper," Digger said.

"Oh."

"And nobody but you knew I was going up there," he said.

"I didn't—"

"I know you didn't," he said. "But the person you told about me did. It was Harker, wasn't it?"

"I…"

"Harker," Digger repeated. "He was the one who gave you that black eye, wasn't he? When he found out you and I were up here playing house the other night. You think he wouldn't shoot at me?"

"I guess he would. He's jealous as a house dog," she said.

"You didn't know he was going to try to kill me, did you?"

She shook her head from side to side. "After I met you the other day, I told Lem about it. He wanted me to keep an eye on you. That's why I came up here, but when I told him about it later, he knew that…well, we had slept together. That's when he hit me. Today…" She shrugged. "I called him when you left the restaurant. What's going on?"

Digger ignored the question. "What's Harker's relationship with Lucius Belton?"

"He's close to Belton. Sometimes he fills in for his chauffeur, and sometimes he's like his bodyguard when Belton's going out of town. What's this all about?"

"I was wondering how Harker knew so much about me so soon," Digger said. "I didn't figure it out until today when I found out his name was Lem. I remembered seeing it on your wristwatch. Where's Harker now?"

"He's waiting for me at my house," she said. "What should I do? I don't want to get involved in any shooting."

"You go home now. Tell him as much as you want. It's up to you," Digger said. "And give him a message for me."

"What's that?"

"Tell him he shouldn't have missed today. Because now I'm going to get him."

Koko was asleep. Digger's tape recorder and the gold-frog microphone were on the table, and propped against them was a note. "Play the recorder," it said.

Digger turned down the volume control and pressed the recorder's "on" button. Koko's soft voice spilled from the machine:

"I don't know if it annoys me more knowing you are out tupping some woman or having to listen to their insipid voices on this stupid machine. You should be lucky that you've got me because everybody else you deal with is a loser.

"Anyway, I listened to all these jerk-off tapes. You should talk to Dolly. Remember her? She's the one with the pneumatic jugs that you picked up in some disgusting saloon.

"If it wasn't Cody Lord or somebody connected with him that went up the cabin to peg shots at you, it was Dolly or somebody she told. Who else knew? Check her out, but not too carefully. I know you've already sampled the goods and once ought to be enough. Why are you so nuts about knockers, anyway?

"Oh, yes, don't bother me when you get in bed. I've got my period. I think I will have it for the next year. Go to hell, you half-breed bastard."

The voice stopped and Digger turned the tape off.

Chapter Seventeen

DIGGER'S LOG:

Tape Recording Number Five, 2:00 A.M. Sunday, recorded in the lap of luxury at the mammoth recording studios of Motel City, Julian Burroughs in the matter of Vernon Gillette.

No new tapes for the master file. Against my better judgment, I left my tape recorder here with Koko, and she listened to all my tapes and now she's mad at me. She's sleeping, but she made it plain that she is jealous of the women I meet at work. She's just lucky I don't work in BSLI's main office. If you want to talk about women, there are women. There are so many women that sometimes one of them will even look longingly at Walter Brackler. Jealous? Hah! What about Hungo Stockyarder? How quickly the woman forgets.

Anyway, what interesting things have happened since last time? That goddamn gorilla cop was staking out Gus's, and I wonder what would have happened if he had found me. That's why we're here, and I'm going to double-bill the company for two rooms. It's bad enough he shoots at me 'cause nobody cares, but if he shoots at Koko, he's going to have ten thousand samurai relatives of hers wrapping bandannas around their heads and taking their swords out of the closet and coming up here to chop him into stir-fried cop. Led by me.

All right. He shot at me. And a cop's car was near the cabin the night Gillette got killed. And Lem Harker is Lucifer Belton's stooge. I would make book right now on Harker killing Gillette at Belton's orders, but, please God, would somebody tell me why? Koko was right. Dolly sicced him on me.

Can you imagine Louise Gillette still wondering, after her husband's dead six months, whether he was having an affair or not? What does it matter if he was banging everybody in western Pennsylvania who managed to escape Hugo whatever-his-name-is? But women like to know things like that just so they can make their lives miserable. It's very strange.

At least, Gillette went out with a bang. But Marla said there wasn't any rug on the floor in front of the beds. That means it was probably put there to hide those burn marks. Why? And the lamp worked.

I'll think about all this tomorrow.

Expenses. Sending a cab to pick up Koko, fifteen dollars round trip. A hundred to Gus LaGrande to rent his car. Fifty dollars for miscellaneous drinks with various witnesses. Forty dollars for this room. Total, two hundred and five.

I don't know what I'm going to do tomorrow. I'm dead-ended, I think, and maybe I'll just pack it all in and leave here and let the home office give everything to the state police and let them figure it out. I don't want to be shot at again.

Me or Koko.

Chapter Eighteen

Digger undressed and went to bed. As he smoked a cigarette in the dark room, he decided that Dolly had probably told Harker what Digger had said. And there was a chance that Harker was now prowling the dark streets of Belton, like a vampire bat, looking for Digger. He might spot and recognize Gus LaGrande's car. So Digger decided he would stay awake all night in case the lunatic found them and came bursting into Digger's room. He would protect Koko at all costs.

He was very proud of this decision and thought of it a lot until he fell asleep five minutes after putting out his cigarette.

He slept soundly, interrupted only by a dream in which Koko did something very nice to him.

When Digger awoke, he reached a hand out to stroke Koko, but the bed was empty. He looked around nervously for a moment, then saw the tape recorder on the pillow next to his head. He lit a cigarette, then pressed the recorder's playback button and Koko's syruped voice filled the room.

"Dear Schmuck. I didn't want to wake you up because you looked like you had a hard night. I listened to your fresh tape and I think you're right. Belton's behind all this, but why? Anyhow, I've got an idea and so I'm going out for a while. Don't worry, nobody in town knows me, and if all these people on your tapes are any sample of the population, I don't want them to get to know me. I'll be all right. Yes, yes, yes. I'll drive slowly. I'd call you before I come back but there's no phone in our room, in case you hadn't noticed, and I didn't want you to have to walk all the way to Phone City to take a call.

"By the way, that was me during the night. I hope it was as good for you as it was for me."

Digger turned off the recorder and looked at his watch. It was almost noon. Women always did that. They didn't ever tell you what time it was when they were leaving a message. He once had a tape machine on his telephone but he finally took it out because it was annoying coming home and finding a message that said, "I'll be over in a minute," and he didn't know what hour it was when the phone call was made. Or even what day, for that matter, because one of the nice things about phone tape machines was that you didn't ever have to go home.

He never did that. He was always very precise on the telephone. He always said, "This is Julian Burroughs. It is now eleven A.M., Tuesday, June twenty-second, in the year of our Lord nineteen eighty-two, and where the fuck are you?"

Digger took a shower, then tried the television, but there were only three channels and they were filled with evangelists intent on proving by Queegian logic that the earth was younger than the rocks it contained.

He sat and smoked cigarettes until 12:45, when he heard a sound at the door. Koko pushed open the door and said, "Hi, Digger. I'm glad you're dressed. Let's go."

"Hold on. Where are we going?"

"Mrs. Gillette's house."

"Why? I don't want to go. I'm having a nice time sitting here, watching the wallpaper peel."

"Let's go," Koko said. "Wear your tape."

She let Digger drive. "Where have you been?" he asked.

"Helping out at the well-baby examinations," she said. "Tell me about Lucius Belton."

"What about him?"

"Is he really as bad as you said on your tapes?" she asked.

"Worse," Digger said. "He's as old as death. His fingers are blue and that means his heart isn't working right."

"His wife's young," Koko said.

"Yeah. It's almost obscene. This isn't June-December; it's more

like B.C.-A.D. I don't think it's one of the big sex relationships of
all time. He looks like his last orgasm was powder. What do you
want to know for?"

He parked the car in front of Louise Gillette's house and saw
that Cody Lord's red pickup truck was parked in the driveway.

"The truck belongs to Gillette's friend," Digger said. "The one
who's sleeping with the widow Gillette."

Koko nodded and followed Digger to the front door. He gave
the brass knocker one sharp rap, and the door was opened only a
few seconds later by the ever-present Ardath.

"Hello, Mr. Burroughs," she said.

"Hi, Ardath. This is my friend, Koko."

The little girl extended her hand. "How do you do?" she said.
"You're very beautiful."

"You're very perceptive," Koko said.

"Is your mother in?" Digger said. "We'd like to talk to her."

Ardath lowered her voice. "Cody is here. They're in the kitchen.
I'll tell them you're here."

"Thank you," Digger said.

As Ardath walked down the hall, Koko said to Digger, "That's
the first person I've ever seen you be polite to, without having an
ulterior motive."

"No ulterior motive, my butt," Digger said. "That kid's coming
into a lot of money. I'm hoping she'll adopt me."

Ardath reappeared and with a crook of her finger motioned
them to follow her. She led them into the kitchen, where Cody
and Mrs. Gillette sat over coffee cups at a large round table. Lord
looked embarrassed to see Digger, who nodded at him.

"Mr. Burroughs," Louise Gillette said.

"This is my assistant, Miss Fanucci," Digger said. Mrs. Gillette
nodded to her politely, even while appraising her with the hard,
instant inspection that one beautiful woman gives another. "She
has a couple of questions," Digger said.

"If we can help," Louise said.

"Your husband had a scar on his right hand," Koko said. "How
did he get it?"

"It was a surgical scar," Louise said. "He had a birthmark
removed."

"Sort of red, star-shaped?" Koko asked.

"Yes, that's right. How did you know?"

Koko ignored the question, which impressed Digger because it was exactly the right thing to do.

"Does Ardath have a similar birthmark?" Koko asked.

Mrs. Gillette shook her head. "Apparently, it's male-linked," she said. "Vernon's father had it too."

Suddenly, Digger knew what Koko was up to. The young Oriental woman turned to him and said, "That's all I need, Dig."

"Just a minute," he said. "Mrs. Gillette, Lord, Vern talked about making a big score. Do either of you know what he meant?"

Lord shook his head. Mrs. Gillette said, "No. He would talk about it once in a while, about something that would make us rich enough to leave this town and never look back."

"He never told you what?" Digger asked.

"No. I surmised it was something he was working on at Belton and Sons. But Vern was kind of close-mouthed about most things."

"Yes, I guess he was," Digger said. "Well, thank you, we'll be going now."

"Just a moment," Mrs. Gillette said. "Have you found out anything? Anything that bears on Vern's death?"

"We may have," Digger said, "but it's too early to tell. We'll let you know as soon as we're sure."

"Please do. This is very important to all of us."

Ardath led them back to the front door, and as they left she said to them, "You're doing excellent work."

"How do you know?" Digger said.

"I can tell," the little girl said.

Outside, Koko remarked, "You've made a conquest. Ardath's in love with you."

"I guess it's me or Lord and she'd rather have a male figure around who at least looks like he has a spine. Gillette was the father of the Belton baby, wasn't he?"

Koko stopped and looked at him. "You're smart, you know that?"

"Not as smart as you. You figured it out first," he said.

"When I heard your tapes, I got to wondering about, what do you call him, Lucifer, being the baby's father. Then while you were out sporting last night with different women, I read the Belton paper and found out that Mrs. Belton and baby were going to kick off that well-baby examination today in the school cafeteria. I went down early and signed up as a volunteer. Her baby's got the birthmark on the back of his right hand. The mother tried to keep it covered up, but I was helping Dr. Leonardo and I got a look at it."

"How'd you know it was hereditary?" Digger asked.

"I didn't. Not for sure. But it was almost a precise five-pointed star. When I was at the university, I studied genetics and I did a paper on birthmarks. This just looked like it might be one of them."

"That's why you made Phi Beta Kappa and I became an accountant," Digger said.

"Don't feel bad," Koko said. "You know more about the Bible than I do. On the tape when I heard you talking about Lucifer, the fallen angel, I thought it was from Milton. Not from Isaiah."

"I don't know just the Bible," Digger said. "I know poetry too. And literature. Do you know who wrote 'The Dissertation on Roast Pig'?"

"No. Who?"

"Lamb. You know how I remember that?" he asked.

"No, how?"

"Because it should have been written by Bacon. What business does Lamb have writing about roast pig? My knowledge of things like this is virtually unlimited. Where are we going now?" he said as they got into the car.

"I think you ought to take this car back before LaGrande hands you up for an auto thief. And I think you ought to buy me breakfast."

"Okay."

"And if you're real good, I'll tell you how Gillette was murdered," she said.

Koko was to the world of food what Digger was to the world of alcohol—a world-class competitor who would not be embarrassed by any competition.

The LaGrande Inn had put out a big Sunday brunch, and Koko had stacked two plates full of eggs and sausage and bacon and pancakes and Danish and buttered rolls. Digger had ordered a drink from the bar, and from the food line he had chosen an English muffin from which he had torn a corner to nibble at.

"How'd you find out?" Digger asked. "Go ahead, talk with your mouth full."

"Thank you," she said. "As I said, I volunteered to help Dr. Leonardo at the well-baby thing so I could get a look at Mrs. Belton. Finding that mark on the baby was a bonus."

"How'd you get Leonardo to let you help?"

"Digger, I'm good at this. I smiled at him and wiggled my ass a little. How was he going to pass me up?"

"How indeed?" Digger said. "Hugo never could."

"There weren't too many babies there so it didn't take too long. Anyway, when it was done, I leveled with Leonardo."

"That's a mistake," Digger said. "Never tell anybody the truth. What'd you tell him?"

"I'll keep that in mind from now on. I told him I was your assistant and I got him talking about Vern Gillette's body."

"He talked?"

"Sure he did. Particularly after I told him what an idiot you were, trying to prove that Gillette had died of a heart attack. Sorry, Digger. I had to do that."

Digger said, "My feelings aren't really hurt. You ought to see what I say about you behind your back."

"So, he told me about the autopsy," Koko said. "And the only unusual thing was the two burn marks on Gillette's wrists. They were real burns."

"Just like the two burns in the cabin floor," Digger said.

"Exactly," she said. "That's when I figured out how they did it. Whoever they were."

"Right," Digger said. "It was probably Harker. He slugged Gillette, then he turned off one of the cabin's electric circuits. He stripped the cord off that lamp and plugged it in. Then he put the two end wires in Gillette's hands or under his wrists or something and plugged in the cord. Then he went into the bathroom and turned on the circuit. It was like an electric chair. It fried Gillette and burned the floor."

"That's the way it sounded to me," Koko said.

Digger nodded. "It all makes sense. You didn't tell Leonardo about any of this, did you?"

"Of course not. I flirted with him and promised to come in for an exam tomorrow…My chest hasn't been feeling good."

"It feels good to me," Digger said.

"But I didn't tell him anything," she said.

"Good."

"What do we do now?" Koko asked.

"I don't know," Digger said, sipping his vodka. He tried another bite of his English muffin, but didn't like it. "Let's see what we've got. We've got Vernon Gillette knocking up his boss's wife, and probably the boss finding out about it. That's probably why all the dinner invitations to the Gillettes suddenly stopped. Then we've got Gillette talking about making a big score. Blackmail the boss, who's bananas about carrying on the Belton and Sons line? Sounds logical. Now we've got Gillette going up to the cabin and Cody Lord leaving him alone. We've got Lord and Mrs. Gillette as an entry, but they didn't kill Gillette because Cody's got no balls and Mrs. Gillette wouldn't do it stupidly. Marla spends some of the night with Gillette up at the cabin. They hear a noise, she runs away, she hears voices and a thud. She sees a cop's car alongside the road with nobody in it. Gillette's dead, certainly not by any accident changing a fuse 'cause there weren't any fuses in the cabin. He's got burn marks and there are burn marks on the floor and there's a lamp with the electrical cord ripped out—and I think you're right, somebody just plugged him in like a Christmas tree. I say Harker. And it was Harker—because Dolly told him I was there—who came up to the cabin and tried to blow me away. If it were Cody, he wouldn't have missed. I've seen his trophies. And, besides, Harker is old man Belton's stooge. That's what we've got; what do you think?"

"What do *you* think?" Koko asked.

"I think it's all we're going to get without getting our asses blown off," Digger said. "I don't like the motive for Belton. You'd think there were other ways of dealing with Gillette and blackmail than by killing him. But I don't know how we can find out anymore. They've already shot at me once—their aim's bound to improve. It's not neat and it annoys me, but I think we go back and I tell Frank Stevens about all of it and let him pull strings and get the state police in here and let them work it over."

"You don't like that idea, do you?" Koko asked, between bites of a Danish pastry.

"No. My cowboy soul doesn't want to leave it at that. It doesn't want to give this to the state police. It wants me to go and get Harker and punch his face off and make him confess and then arrest them all and tie it up in a neat little package. But that won't work. First of all, who the hell around here would we get to arrest Harker? He's a town cop. They'll arrest me, but not him. Not on my word."

"You're right," Koko said. She sipped her coffee. "What about Mrs. Gillette's money?"

"I think she'll go along. She wants the killer. If the state cops say murder, she'll get her half mill. If they say no murder, then… ah, shit, then we're right back where we started from, arguing with her about a million or a half million. I hate things that aren't neat and tidy."

"How come you're such a slob then?" Koko asked.

"I try to be neat. It's just not my style," Digger said.

Both her plates were empty and wiped as clean as if they had just come out of a dishwasher. Koko smiled and folded her napkin and said, "Screw it, then, it's settled. Give it to Stevens for the state cops. You and I will enjoy the rest of our weekend. We'll find horses and go riding." She hesitated. "You owe it to Mrs. Gillette, though, to tell her just what's going down."

"Screw the horseback riding," Digger said. "I think we ought to just get out of here before Harker finds another reason to shoot at me. Gunfire can stampede our mounts, podner. But I'll go talk to Mrs. Gillette. She's got to be careful too."

Digger left Koko to pack while he drove, in his own rented car, to Mrs. Gillette's. Cody Lord had gone and Louise listened calmly as Digger went through the story step by step. He left nothing out, and when he was done, she said, "I think you're absolutely right. This is a matter now for police agencies. They've got more resources than you do, and…well, I'm not comfortable with the thought of your being a target."

"Thank you," Digger said. "It makes me uncomfortable too. Where's Ardath?"

"She's out playing."

"Are you going to tell her about this?"

"Yes, of course. Perhaps not every detail, but there isn't any point in trying to hide the truth from her."

"She can handle it," Digger said. "When you talk to her, tell her I did my best. And you both be careful."

"We will," Mrs. Gillette said. "Thank you."

When he got back to his room at Gus LaGrande's, Koko was gone. The suitcases still were not packed, and Digger suspected that after eating a breakfast big enough for four, she had gotten hungry again and gone downstairs for lunch.

But she was not in any of the dining rooms and he asked Gus, on duty behind the bar, "Have you seen the girl I was with?"

"Koko? Yeah, she went running out of here about a half-hour ago. There was a phone call to your room, and a couple of minutes later she came flying out."

"She say anything?"

"No."

"Do you know who called?"

Gus shook his head. "Some guy. I didn't know the voice."

"Who'd he ask for?"

"Oh. Miss Fanucci in Mr. Burroughs' room," Gus said.

Digger nodded. He felt a knot slowly tightening in the pit of his stomach, but he went back upstairs to the room to wait.

Chapter Nineteen

"Burroughs?"

"Yeah, Harker. Where is she?"

"You've got a pretty little girl friend, Burroughs. Very pretty."

"Harker, don't mess around. It's me you want, not her. She doesn't know anything. Now where is she?"

"You just sit your ass right there by the phone, Burroughs. I'm going to call you in exactly one hour. Maybe if you're good, I'll let you talk to her. If she's not otherwise occupied."

"You bastard," Digger said.

"An hour, Burroughs. And if you talk to anybody about anything, well, you're never going to see your little slant again."

Click.

Digger hung up the telephone, which had gone dead in his hand. An hour. Harker was trying to keep him on ice. For what? To have more time to rough up Koko? No. To give them time to set things up to get rid of both Digger and Koko. He had an hour.

Just an hour.

Digger went to his dresser and took out the laundry bag of tape recordings. Into the bag he also dropped the business card of Frank Stevens, the president of BSLI. He took the bag downstairs to Gus.

The bar was empty as Digger handed the bag over.

"Gus, listen, this is important."

"All ears," the young man said.

"If anything happens, there's a business card in this bag. I want you to call that person and tell him you've got this bag. You understand?"

"I guess so. Like what's going to happen?"

"Never mind. If it happens, you'll know it. But this bag doesn't go to anybody except the name on that card. You got it?"

"Right. I got it."

"Gus, do you keep a gun around here?" Digger asked.

"A gun?" The young man hesitated. "Yeah, I keep a little gun. It's a .22 pistol—it ain't worth shit."

"I need it," Digger said.

"I don't like this. What for? I can't go giving anybody my gun."

"Gus, this is life or death. I need that gun. Where is it?"

"I keep it…here under the register."

"Turn your back," Digger said.

The young man did and Digger fished the small pistol from the back of the shelf under the register.

"I just stole your gun," he said. "Tonight when you find it missing, report the theft."

"Hey, what's going on?" Gus asked.

"Later. I'll tell you everything later," Digger said.

"It's Burroughs, isn't it?" There was a large smile on Dr. Leonardo's face as he answered the door after Digger's incessant ringing of the bell. "I met your assistant today."

The smile vanished as Digger stuck the gun into the doctor's ample stomach and pushed him back inside the house. He slammed the door behind him.

"Where are they?"

"Where is who?" Leonardo said.

"Belton, Harker, the girl. Where are they?"

"I don't know what you're talking about," Leonardo said.

"I'm going to tell you once," Digger said. "You met my assistant today. You were the only one who knew she worked with me. Now they've taken her. That's because you told them who she was. Who'd you tell?"

The doctor hesitated and Digger pressed the muzzle of the gun under the doctor's nose. "Who'd you tell?"

"Only Lucius, when I got home."

"Where was he when you talked to him?"

"At his house."

Digger herded the doctor toward the back of the house, to a small private office.

"Pick up that phone. Find out if he's home. That's all I want to know. Don't make any mistakes and don't mention me." He cocked the hammer on the pistol.

Nervously, Leonardo dialed a number from memory.

"Lucius, it's Vince." The doctor nodded to Digger. "Oh. I understand. I'll call you tomorrow. It wasn't important."

He hung up the phone and said to Digger, "He's home. He said he's busy now." Beads of sweat rolled down Leonardo's forehead. "Can you put that gun away? What's this all about?"

"Lie on the floor there," Digger said. He found a roll of surgical tape and taped Leonardo's hands together behind his back. Then he taped his ankles together and pulled them up and fastened the wrist bands to the ankle restraints with even more tape.

"You've got a big mouth, Doctor," Digger said. "How deep were you in it? Did they have you phony up Gillette's autopsy to cover the murder?"

"Murder? I don't know what you're talking about," Leonardo said.

"We're going to find out, aren't we?" Digger said. He put five big strips of tape across the doctor's mouth. "You just stay there and don't you try moving," Digger said. "I'll be back for you. If it hurts, take thirty aspirin and call me in a month."

He ripped the telephone junction box from the wall and then locked the office door behind him. A minute later he was in his car, pedal to the floor, speeding up the side of the bowl toward Lucius Belton's mansion.

Digger parked fifty yards away from the gates of the Belton home, out of sight of the guard booth. He checked his watch. Thirty minutes left before he was due to receive his next phone call from Harker, and suddenly he hoped that the big stupid cop was able to tell time correctly.

Digger walked up to the gate. The guard, a wiry man in his mid-forties, was in the booth reading a magazine.

"Hey, buddy," Digger called. The guard looked up and Digger gestured to him to come to the gate.

"Yeah? What is it?" the guard said.

Digger motioned for him to come closer.

"Is Harker here?" he asked.

"Who wants to know?" the guard said. He was too close, and Digger was able to reach through the bars of the gate and grab the collar of his windbreaker. He pulled the man even closer to the gate and pushed the gun into his face.

"This wants to know," he said.

"He's here. He's here. What do you want?"

"Now here's what you're going to do," Digger said. "I'm going to let go of you. You're going to back up to that booth. Don't take your eyes off me because I'm not taking mine off you. You're going to reach inside that booth and trip the lock on this gate. Fuck up and you're dead. You got it?"

"I got it," the guard said. There was blind terror on his face.

"Do it," Digger said. He released him, and, keeping his eyes locked on Digger's, the guard backed up to the gate house. Just to emphasize the point, Digger cocked the pistol and kept it pointed at the man's chest. Carefully, the man reached inside the shack. His hand fumbled with something.

"No tricks," Digger said. "You're not faster than a speeding bullet." He heard a click in the gate lock in front of him, pushed the gate open and slipped inside.

"Is that the only way it unlocks?" Digger asked.

"Yes."

"No keys—just the electric lock release?"

"Yes. That's right."

"When's your relief coming?"

"Not till four o'clock. Two hours."

"All right," Digger said. "Go out through that gate and start walking down that road ahead of me." He herded the man through the gate, first propping it open with a stone. At his car, he opened the trunk and ordered the man to crawl inside.

"You're kidding. I'll die in there," the guard said.

"Maybe," Digger said coldly. "But you'll surely die out here. Get inside."

The man clambered in and Digger slammed the trunk lid closed, then ran back to the gate. Once inside the grounds, he closed the gate and heard it click shut again.

The Belton home stood at the top of a hill. The long driveway curved up toward the house and then looped back down to rejoin the roadway about fifty yards from the gate.

If he went up the roadway, Digger thought, he'd stand out like ink on a white shirt, so he cut off into the trees that bordered the right side of the roadway and ran through them toward the back of the house. As he got close to the house, he heard dogs barking and he felt a chill at the base of his neck. But as he turned the corner of the house he saw that the dogs, four German shepherds, were enclosed in a kennel behind the house. They snarled and growled as Digger drew close, but he ignored them, stooping low below the level of the windows as he ran along the back of the house.

Twenty-two minutes left.

At the far corner of the house, Digger saw a large, open garage-type door. It led to a storage area that probably once housed an old carriage. A door in the corner of the area led to the house. Digger looked through the small glass windows in the door. A hallway stretched in front of him. The doorway was unlocked and he opened it and stepped inside. He paused for a moment, but heard nothing and started down the hall. He was in the wing of the house that served as quarters for Belton's domestic staff. On the left side of the hallway were small bedrooms and a tiny parlor. To the right, there was a large kitchen, but there were no sounds coming from it. Digger remembered it was Sunday; perhaps the Belton workers had been given the day off.

The hallway ended at a small flight of steps, and Digger took them two at a time. The stairway stopped with a door, and Digger listened at it for a moment, before opening it carefully. He was in the main entrance hall of the Belton home. Still he heard and saw no one.

The long, wide hallway, lined with oil paintings, led off to the right and Digger moved quietly along it. Behind a set of closed double doors, he heard voices, and he moved his ear close to the door.

He heard Koko's voice:

"I don't know what you're talking about."

And Belton's:

"It's too late for lying, miss."

And Harker's:

"It doesn't matter. We're going to take care of everything in a while anyway. It won't matter what you know."

Digger cocked the hammer of the .22 pistol in his hand, then released it gently. He had forgotten to look to see if Gus's damn gun was loaded. He checked the cylinders and saw the brass bases of shells. He recocked the gun and gently turned the doorknob. It turned smoothly and he felt the door start to move open.

Thinking, here goes nothing, he took a deep breath, slammed the door open and jumped into the room.

Belton was sitting behind a desk in the far corner, Koko sat on a chair facing him across the desk and Harker stood behind her.

"Hold it!" Digger shouted.

Harker spun around and his hand went toward the holster on his hip.

"Koko, duck," Digger yelled, and the young Oriental woman dove onto the floor. Harker hesitated.

Digger said, "Try it, Harker. I won't need much excuse to kill you where you stand."

Harker stared at Digger for a second, then let his hand drop limply to his side.

"Turn around, you stupid shit," Digger said. "Face that wall." Harker did as he was ordered and Digger stepped up behind him and took his gun from his holster.

It felt sturdier, more businesslike in his hand, and he replaced Gus's gun in his pocket and with the barrel of Harker's gun, slapped the big uniformed cop across the skull behind his ear. Harker groaned and his legs buckled for a moment. "That's for nothing," Digger said.

He then turned and pointed the gun at Belton, who sat at the desk, his sickly colored hands clenched into fists.

"Get out from behind there," Digger ordered. He glanced around the office. There was a sofa under bookshelves across the room from Belton's desk. "Both of you, move over there. Sit on that couch." He herded them with the point of the big pistol while he asked Koko, "You all right?"

"I'm fine," she said.

"They didn't hurt you?"

"Not yet. They were planning to. Both of us."

"It's get-even time," Digger said. "Get on the phone and call the state police. Tell them you're reporting a murder and get them up here. Tell them no local cops." As he turned back to Belton and Harker, sitting uncomfortably on the small sofa like two ugly bookends, he transferred the pistol to his left hand and casually reached inside his jacket to turn on his tape recorder.

"She doesn't have to call the police," Belton said. "I'm sure we can come to some kind of understanding."

"You mean money?" Digger said.

"Of course. A great deal of money."

"Fuck him, Digger," said Koko. "They were going to take us up the cabin tonight and burn it down with us in it. And the fat bastard called me a slant."

"You heard the lady," Digger said. "You should have known better than to cross a Japanese woman. They never forgive and they never forget."

"But this is all a misunderstanding," Belton said. His pasty-white face had reddened, Digger noticed, and he was working his hands together in his seat. Harker held a hand to the bruise on his skull. His little pig eyes glared hatred.

"Just like it was a misunderstanding when you sent this gorilla up to the cabin to kill Gillette?" Digger said. "What was it, Belton? Was he trying to blackmail you? Or couldn't you just stand the idea anymore that he was the father of your kid?"

He heard Koko's voice ask the operator for the number of the nearest state police barracks. The old man heard her too.

"Please," Belton said. "Let's talk. We can work this all out."

"You talk, I'm listening," Digger said. "Hold the call," he told Koko. "Now I want the truth." He wanted it on tape.

"Vernon Gillette's dead," Belton said. "Nothing can bring him back now."

"He's dead and you ordered him killed," Digger said.

The old man hesitated. "Yes. Okay. Yes, I did. He was blackmailing me. After I had gone to so much trouble selecting him. He seemed just right and…"

Something clicked in Digger's mind. "Selecting him? For what?"

The old man didn't answer.

"Gillette didn't seduce your wife. You and your wife seduced *him*. You hired him to father a kid for you. That's why you had all those physical tests, sperm counts, IQ tests, all that examination crap you ran on him for three days. You weren't hiring an executive— you were hiring a father."

Belton was silent and Digger shouted, "That's right, isn't it?"

"All right," the old man snarled. "Yes. That's right."

"Did Gillette know that he was being hired to service your wife?"

"No. Amanda and I, well, we just made it possible for the two of them to be together and she seduced him. I wanted that baby, Mr. Burroughs. To carry on the line."

"And then you were afraid he was going to shake you down, and you killed him. You had this moron go up and electrocute him. Isn't that right?"

Belton was silent, and Digger took a step toward Harker and raised the pistol as if to slap the cop across the face with it. "Talk, you creepy fuck."

"Yeah, yeah. That's right," Harker said. "He told me to do it."

"But you had fun doing it, didn't you?" Digger said. "Whose brilliant idea was it to bring an electrical fuse up there? To a cabin that didn't use fuses?"

Harker looked pained and Belton shook his head. Then the old man leaned forward.

"How much do you want, Burroughs? How much?"

"You don't have that much money, Belton," said Digger. "Koko, make that call. I want this dimwit for murder, and Belton...I want you for a half-dozen things—murder, conspiracy to commit, kidnapping my assistant, probably a half dozen other charges, including impersonating a father. And a man."

The old man's face strained at the boundary between red and purple. The cords on his fragile neck stood out. He roared, "You can't talk to me like that."

"I'll talk to you any way I want, you impotent old bastard," Digger growled.

There was another voice and Digger turned to see Amanda Belton standing in the doorway of the room.

She was staring at her husband. "You had Vern murdered?" she said.

Belton looked down at the floor.

"Answer me," she screamed.

He was silent, and Digger said, "Maybe the cat's got his tongue."

She walked over to her husband and stood alongside the small sofa. "He's right," she screamed. "You are an impotent old bastard. And a fucking murderer. Lucius, you son of a bitch." She turned to Digger. "Whatever your name is, get the police here. I'll testify against this son of a bitch. I hope he fries. And when he does, I'm going to inherit that entire goddamn company, and you know what I'm going to do? I'm going to take my son, *my* son, goddammit, and I'm going to change his name to Gillette. And then I'm going to change the name of the company to Gillette. Lucius…fucking murder?" She shook her head as if mystified.

"You'll do nothing like that," Belton shouted. "He's my son. And it's my company."

"Not anymore," Amanda said. "Not anymore."

Belton hopped to his feet, his face twisted with rage and fury. Suddenly, his body seemed to shake uncontrollably and his face contorted. He clapped both hands to the center of his chest. His eyes looked as if they were going to burst from their deep sockets.

"You can't…" he rasped from deep back in his throat, and then he fell. He hit the carpet face first and then crumpled onto his side. His eyes were wide open, staring at nothing and at everything. Instinctively, Amanda Belton started to his side, when Harker leaped off the sofa and threw his arm around Mrs. Belton's neck. He turned her so that she was between him and Digger like a shield.

"You're so goddamn smart, Burroughs, aren't you? Go ahead. Shoot. Kill her. Go ahead."

He dragged the woman toward the door to the office. Digger pointed the gun in their direction, but he knew that he could not fire for fear of hitting the woman.

"How far you going to get, Harker?" Digger asked.

"Anyplace away from here," Harker said. He was in the doorway now. He stepped back through the doorway, pushed Mrs. Belton toward Digger and fled down the hall.

"In a pig's ass," Digger said. He turned to Koko, who was just hanging up the telephone. She looked as cool as an executive's secretary who had just finished booking him an airline flight.

"They're on their way," she said.

"Take care of Mrs. Belton," Digger said. He reached into his pocket and pulled out Gus's small pistol. He dropped it into Koko's hand and said, "Here. Shoot anybody who pesters you." Then he turned and ran out the door.

Harker's police car was already speeding down the driveway when Digger got outside. He looked around and saw the Mercedes Benz limousine parked in the circular drive. The keys were in it, and Digger started it up, dropped the automatic shift lever into "drive" and sped off around the circular parking area. Down at the gates, he saw that Harker's green-and-yellow prowl car had stopped and that the cop was getting out to go to the booth to unlock the gates. Digger stepped on the gas harder as the cop vanished into the booth. A split second later Harker peered out, saw the onrushing Mercedes Benz and raised a pistol.

Damn, Digger thought. I should have known he'd have another gun in the car.

Harker stood in the doorway of the booth, firing at the speeding limousine. Digger heard two bullets ping off the metal body of the car and then the windshield went star-burst crazed as a bullet hit it. Digger spun the wheel and aimed the big armored sedan at the guard booth. It hit with a thump and then a cracking sound of wood. He saw Harker's body flying through the air and landing in a lump on the grass, five feet away.

Digger stopped the limousine and walked over to the cop. He was conscious and groaning, and when he saw Digger standing over him, he hissed, "You bastard."

Digger rolled him over with his toe, removed the policeman's handcuffs from the back of his belt and handcuffed a wrist and ankle behind his back. He stood up and looked down at his handiwork, pleased with the day's work.

"All's well that ends well," Digger said and then strolled back toward the house.

Digger had just finished explaining everything to a state police lieutenant, who managed to look confused and annoyed at the same time. They were in another room in the Belton home, along with Koko and Mrs. Belton.

"And that's it, Lieutenant," Digger said. "Mrs. Belton will confirm everything I said. And I guess Harker will too."

"I hate complicated cases like this," the lieutenant said.

"A man after my own heart," Digger said, and then a thought occurred to him.

"Lieutenant, how long can a person live in the trunk of a car?"

"I don't know. Why?"

"'Cause the gatekeeper's in the trunk of my car. It's parked on the road outside," Digger said.

"Jesus Christ. Is there anything else you've done today to screw up Pennsylvania?"

"Well, there's one thing," Digger said. "There's this doctor in town. I've got him tied up and he ought to be getting pretty muscle-sore about now."

Driving back to Gus's LaGrande Inn, Digger told Koko, "Well, I hope you've enjoyed your weekend with me in the country."

"Ahhh, the weekend's over already and we didn't get a chance to go horseback riding," she said.

Digger sighed. "I know. That's the way it is, though. Time flies when you're having fun."

Chapter Twenty

"This is Julian Burroughs, let me talk to Brackler."

"Just a moment, I'll see if he's in."

"Of course he's in—let me talk to him."

"Just a moment, sir, I'll see."

"I hope you give good head, because your telephone technique is crapola."

"I beg your pardon. What did you say?"

"Eight times I said, let me talk to Kwash. *That* you don't hear. Once I make a personal comment and suddenly you've got bat ears. Let me talk to Kwash."

"I'll see if he's in."

"Kwash, how much money did I save the company up in Belton?"

"Well, you might say—"

"Might say, my ass. I saved you guys five hundred thousand dollars."

"All right. So what?"

"Then why did you cut down my expense check?"

"Digger, I've seen the way you dress. Don't tell me that that ripped jacket cost four hundred fifty dollars and your trousers cost two hundred. Your whole wardrobe isn't worth six hundred fifty dollars."

"Not if you're talking about resale value," Digger said. "But there are other kinds of value."

"You're telling me this jacket and pants had sentimental value?" Walter Brackler said.

"Yes, goddammit, they were a gift from my mother. She bought the jacket at Jacket City. The pants from Pants City. They're irreplaceable. From my mother, God rest her soul."

"Your mother's still alive; I saw her last month."

"Then God rest my soul," Digger said.

"I'll give you a hundred bucks for the set," Brackler said.

"That's ridiculous. Today, you can hardly buy a pair of pants for a hundred dollars. Much less a jacket."

"*You* can," Brackler said. "A hundred bucks."

"Three hundred," Digger said. "Not a penny less."

"Two hundred. Take it or leave it."

"You're a hard man, Kwash."

"Take it or leave it."

"You've got no soul," Digger said.

"Two hundred. That's it."

"I'll take it," Digger said.

"I have this feeling I'm still being robbed," Brackler said.

"Best bargain you've ever made," Digger said. "Those garments were irreplaceable."

When he hung up the telephone, Koko called out from the kitchen of their Las Vegas condominium, "How'd you make out?"

"He cheated me out of four hundred and fifty dollars," Digger said.

"You'll get even," she said.

"You bet I will." He lay in bed, smoking a cigarette, then picked up the telephone again, got a number from information and dialed.

"Hello, Flower City? This is Digger. I know, I know, your name's not Flower City. I was thinking of something else. I'm okay. You? Good. Listen, I want to send some flowers to somebody. Yes. Her name is Ardath Gillette." He gave the address in Belton, Pennsylvania. "How much? Okay. Send her four hundred and fifty dollars' worth of flowers. That's right. Four hundred and fifty. Yeah. Right. And bill them to my company account. Right. That's Brokers Surety Life Insurance. Thanks. No card. Be sure to mark the bill to the attention of Walter Brackler."

About the Author

Warren Murphy was born in Jersey City, New Jersey. He worked in journalism, editing, and politics. After many of his political colleagues were arrested, Murphy took it as a sign that he needed to find a new career and the Destroyer series was born. Murphy has five children—Deirdre, Megan, Brian, Ardath, and Devin—and a few grandchildren. He has been an adjunct professor at Moravian College, Bethlehem, Pennsylvania, and has also run workshops and lectured at many other schools and universities. His hobbies are golf, mathematics, opera, and investing. He has served on the board of the Mystery Writers of America and has been a member of the Private Eye Writers of America, the International Association of Crime Writers, the American Crime Writers League, and the Screenwriters Guild.

Warren Murphy's website is www.warrenmurphy.com.

OPEN ROAD
INTEGRATED MEDIA

Open Road Integrated Media is a digital publisher and multimedia content company. Open Road creates connections between authors and their audiences by marketing its ebooks through a new proprietary online platform, which uses premium video content and social media.